Mary R. L Bryce

Memoir of John Veitch

Mary R. L Bryce

Memoir of John Veitch

ISBN/EAN: 9783337399917

Printed in Europe, USA, Canada, Australia, Japan

Cover: Foto ©Raphael Reischuk / pixelio.de

More available books at **www.hansebooks.com**

MEMOIR

OF

JOHN VEITCH, LL.D.

PROFESSOR OF LOGIC AND RHETORIC
UNIVERSITY OF GLASGOW

BY

MARY R. L. BRYCE

WILLIAM BLACKWOOD AND SONS
EDINBURGH AND LONDON
MDCCCXCVI

PREFACE.

THIS outline of Professor Veitch's life is given to his friends with all diffidence, and no small sense of responsibility. It was undertaken at Mrs Veitch's request, and subject to her approval, and carried out with the assistance of my sister, Lindsay H. Wilson, in gathering and arranging material.

To all those who so liberally gave me help, and intrusted manuscript and reminiscence to my judgment, I am deeply indebted.

Especially I desire to thank Emeritus Professor Campbell Fraser, Professor Knight, Professor Calderwood, Rev. Dr Williamson, Professor Ramsay, and Mr Taylor Innes.

The imperfect realisation of what had weight and true bearing in the life we study, is often urged as a reason against venturing upon biographical ground. One simple source of failure may perhaps lie in faulty affection, which by its nature is incapable of discernment. Be that as it may, I am well aware that the only claim I can make upon the readers of my uncle's life is that of deep affection for him, and the memory of a friendship of many years and of close sympathy, the value and the happiness of which — to me — cannot be set down in words.

MARY R. L. BRYCE.

GLASGOW, *September* 1896.

CONTENTS.

ILLUSTRATIONS.

MEMOIR OF JOHN VEITCH

PART I.

BIGGIESKNOWE

BIGGIESKNOWE.

PERHAPS in no way is the responsibility of life more convincingly brought home to us than when we search back for light upon the development, for explanation of the powers, of the unit among his fellow-men. But unless prompted by sincerity, admiration, and love, this search becomes mere inquisitiveness, and a degenerate task.

As we handle yellowed pages, letters from the dead to our dead, and con over the hitherto hidden things; when, sifted out before us, these lie open, which were never meant for our eye; then the delicacy and strangeness of the task of giving them to others is besetting indeed. The doubt may even make itself felt as to what justification there is for the unasked-for candour, this unveiling of the forgotten and the personal. To some minds there is none.

Yet when the life has been great according to its opportunities, mastering and surmounting as it went on, it is natural to look back upon every phase with reverence and interest. Indeed this interest is simply a form of faith in our kind, answering also the desire which all men share to be "remembered for good." The mystery is not less because we have a key in our hand to the growth of a mind and the making of a character. Rather, holding that key, shall we pause on the threshold, and guard our spirit of inquiry by the charm too deep ever to become old-fashioned,—in the beginning God made him.

To the life of John Veitch attaches a subtle attraction, though no stirring scenes break in upon the picture of it, and many of its periods are sounded in a minor, even monotonous key. For it simply arose, like any of the nature-forces with which he was in such intimate sympathy, and whose processes are hidden from the common eye.

That there ran in his veins the blood of one of the fiercest and finest of Border races there can be no doubt ; and that there existed in his temperament, his physique, in certain of his tenets, and habits of mind, the bias of a son of the soil, is equally evident. These elements were striking, not in antithesis but in com- bination ; they made up a man who was in reality of no class, though he shared, on occasion, the prejudices of two ; they granted to him a catholicity of temper unusual in a Scot so vividly and passionately Scottish.

" I like to see the mothers of men I like." It was in a letter to her son that Dr John Brown [1] thus refers to Mrs Veitch, senior ; and we have some touching allusions to her both in the son's letters and his verses. There are those who remember her as already past her prime, but still obviously a woman of character and force ; physically and mentally robust ; her memory stored with the romantic lore of the country- side. Her face would light up, even after stricken by a form of palsy, on recalling or hearing an amusing incident. Her sisters, " Tibbie" and " Ailie," were not women of the simple power of Nancy Ritchie, the maiden name by which, in Scottish custom, Mrs Veitch

[1] Author of 'Rab and his Friends.'

was all her life known. She married late,
being at least thirty, and John was her first-
born. Indeed we may think of him as her
only child, for although an infant brother died,
and a sister lived to be a bright child of seven,
he alone was her pride and solace. His own
words speak to his feeling for her :—

> ". . . Whose life was flow'ring of a noble heart,
> To whom self-sacrifice was natural
> As is the living breath of heaven's own air.
> Her hand was busy as the day was long,
> And in her eyes the mute appealing look
> Of any creature God had made awoke
> Deep sympathy; the harebell on rude bank
> Between her fields was to her heart a joy.
> And imaged clear in memory I see
> The slender waving grass of autumn days
> She plucked and set above the mantelpiece
> Quaint figured; there all through the winter-time
> To wear its grace, till living touch of spring
> Quickened anew the beauty of the year." [1]

Fully ten years before these lines were published, John Veitch wrote to his college friend,
Alexander Nicolson, on hearing of a visit
which the latter had paid to the old people
at Biggiesknowe. The unwilling absentee
says : "Your call on the old folks could not
have been but flattering to them, and agree-

---

[1] The Tweed, p. 36.

able, especially when they found the frank and large-hearted man with whom they had to do — a particular this which my mother (God bless her!) would soon discover, for to some of the rarest qualities of womanhood she adds keen discriminative observation."

Dr John Brown visited her in his double capacity of friend and doctor, and wrote after the visit, with certain data about her illness, adding : "I hope you may have her long with you. I saw you looking out from her face, and I don't wonder at all your love for and to her. She got to my heart by repeating my father's text at Mossfennan after my mother's death." (The text was, "So I spake unto the people in the morning; and at even my wife died"![1]) "There are few such people now in the world; they are like old houses; their walls bearing marks of the inroads and the blasts of time; the walls thick, and *therefore* warm, and the central fire burning bright and strong and clear far in." It is true : even in the old faded photograph one still sees him looking out from her face.

From his mother John Veitch gets the thin-

[1] Ezekiel, xxiv. 18.

lipped stern mouth, the blunt nose and strong
eyebrows, but the forehead is in his case filled
out to new and noble proportions, and eyes
such as his are not inherited. No one who
had seen them while he rebuked some brutal
man urging an overladen horse, or when he
lifted up his voice and recited on the moors,
or when his glance rested on the face of a
friend, could forget that flash, that intensity,
that softened blue depth.

Another faded photograph presents to the
younger generation the old man James Veitch,
who is still remembered in Peebles as Sergeant
Veitch, or "Veitch the Fisher." He stands,
his withered kindly face bent before strong
sunshine, with rod in one hand and a bonnie
trout from his basket in the other. It is
curious to note how exactly he gave his
hands to his son : shape and character seem
identical; but beyond that there is small
likeness. One can hardly imagine from the
picture that this easy-going old angler was
once a soldier; yet so it was, and perhaps it
is as true a tribute as we could find to the
power of the Border country over her sons,
that the very look of the soldier, generally

so deeply engrained, seems to have fallen from him. He continued all through later life to haunt the Tweed and its streams, and to instruct ambitious boys in the art he delighted in. It was James Veitch who knew the best pools, and the very nature of fish and fly.

A little anecdote remains of how he cured his small John of an ardent desire to bathe in Tweed. As every one knows, as he certainly knew, Tweed is dangerous for bathers, and many a child has been lost in it. John, a youngster of about six, was "craiking" (*i.e.*, pleading and whimpering in one) to be allowed a dip. "Come with me," quoth the father. They reached an apparently suitable spot. "Off with your clothes!" The child obeyed and went in, but, alas! the water proved at once too deep. So, by stern command, on went the garments again, and, discouraged, the boy followed his father to another place. "Take off your clothes now." The boy did so, but here the water was much too shallow. The clothes were donned once more, and the poor little urchin followed as before. A third time he had to endure discomfiture; the stones were too sharp or the current too strong. He

was for ever cured of his craving; but perhaps
there and then began his intimate knowledge
of the varied and fascinating river, for which he
grew to have such ineffaceable love. There is
something in the dry patient humour of this
form of discipline quite in keeping with the
kindliness and hardihood of the early home
life.

From the mouth of Mr John Keddie, a
Peebles octogenarian, and a former provost
of the royal burgh, we have a lively picture
of the little family in the Biggiesknowe cottage. "Being thirteen year aulder than the
Professor, ye may see, I mind him fine as a
wee laddie. . . . Ay, she was a very 'cute
woman, Mistress Veitch, the mother; and as
for James Veitch, he was a genial nice man,
that everybody likit; no kind o' kink [double-
ness] about him." He was, it seems, "full o'
stories," and though not "a furious auld
Scotchman," was proud to wear his Peninsular medal in the front pew of the "Hammer-
men's loft" in the Established Church, dividing
himself on this loyal occasion from both wife
and son; for "think ye, would he gang to
the Free Kirk wi' it on his breist?" On one

occasion, according to Dr Williamson, there was no service in the parish church, and the sergeant was persuaded to go to the Free with his wife and son. But he would only do so in his private capacity as a citizen and without his medal. Proud too was he to relate tales of his numerous battles; proudest of all to have seen service under Wellington. He was a "weel set-up auld soldier," noted as good company. And the contrast of John's staid and studious habit seems to have struck the old residenter. Many a time had he noticed the little boy "aye runnin' aboot, wi' his buik at his airm, a canty callant!"

John was twenty-eight when his father died, and thirty-seven when he lost his mother; but, long before they passed away, he stood out from among his old surroundings, and entered the sphere to which his fitness was his sole and adequate passport. However derived, the boy showed from the earliest a robust force, a methodical energy of mind and body; a singleness of purpose, an instinct for the best within his reach, which drew the attention of discerning eyes, and even stirred local prophets to utterance. As a child in arms he had vivid single impressions, which, he said, never lost hold on his matured imagination. One was of crossing water in some one's arms; another of seeing a negro's face against bright sunshine, and being horrified.

Nothing is more characteristic of him than his conduct at the infant school, which, at seven, he left of his own accord, after three years' attendance, remarking to his mother, "That man can teach me no more," and adding that he had placed himself at another school; which indeed was fact. There was a kind of frank egotism in this juvenile performance which was often attributed to him both by friends and adversaries in after-life. Perhaps it was due, for it cannot be denied, to something subtler than mere self-consciousness or self-esteem. Untoward or novel circumstances would often bring out the one; minds foreign to his peculiar bias would at times call up a spirit of domination, and blind both sides to common qualities, in an unfortunate degree.

Mr Smith, to whom we owe a kind letter of reminiscence, himself remembers how, when he started his Adventure school in Peebles, one of the six scholars who enrolled on the opening day, 20th November 1837, was John Veitch, the independent boy of eight who "placed himself" and told afterwards. He was not many months in showing his quality, and his master, observing his thoughtfulness, diligence, and determination, began early to perceive his native distinction and to hope good things of him. As his first year at the Adventure school drew to a close, John was no longer one of six, but one among a hundred and six pupils. He worked the better, however, under the stimulus of numbers, and "stood well," says Mr Smith, "in all his classes." Bible-lessons began the school work of each day, and afterwards the children were questioned on given passages. John thoroughly enjoyed this, and was ever ready with quick answer. He had an attentive habit, and exceptional powers of memory. Half only of Saturday was holiday for the boys, and the mornings were devoted to recitations, repetition of Psalms, and what was called "Questions." This last meant, that after the first boy had answered the first question, he in turn put the second to his neighbour, and so on through the school. In these Saturday

lessons John excelled, especially in recitation;
his delivery of parts of Scott's poems, "an'
they things" (!), is still held in remembrance,
and the faculty grew as he matured.

After just two years at the "beggarly elements," he was advised by his master to begin
Latin, that kind and wise friend promising help
and encouragement if the child took his advice.
A year later, "he had mastered the grammar
and could already read in our Latin authors,"
as his teacher tells, "with ease and correctness."

Mr Smith speaks of having had a "great
respect" for the boy as one of his scholars.
Certain it is that mingled gratitude, affection,
and respect existed all through after-years in
the mind of his pupil. In 1886, having occasion to write to Mr Smith on his ministerial
jubilee, this feeling is thus expressed: "I owe
you much as my teacher. I have not forgot
the time when I conned my lessons under your
eye, or the mental quickening I derived from
your valuable instructions." Presently Mr
Smith left the town, and the next step for
John Veitch was to the old grammar-school of
Peebles, first under Mr Sloan, and subsequently
two other masters. There he remained until,

at sixteen, he became a student in the University of Edinburgh. Of the grammar-school period, which extended over four to five years, we learn little that is really new. No doubt they were important and precocious years; but the record of his conduct has consistence all along, and nothing fresh can be noted of his outstanding force, and of his fashion of grasping with purpose and result whatever occupied him.

Out of doors, and out of school, his studious ways were flung aside. He did not take much part in the ordinary (or shall we say extraordinary?) games of the school, although joining his comrades faithfully enough at "ispy," "bools," and "shinty." But he never had any liking or aptitude for games. His real pastime was fishing, in which his father early tutored him; and his friends must remember many a time when he recounted in his vivid way the pranks he played, the pure delight it was to him to act truant from home with his rod, and to wander, to his mother's great anxiety, till after nightfall, even till one in the morning, up the lovely recesses of the Border streams.

Often, however, when play-hour came, John was either at work or pacing up and down the green, just as if thinking out some matter. And when we picture the little boy already pondering and pacing the green the while, we see again the grey-haired man, who always liked a long uncrowded room, where, as he worked and studied, he would walk to and fro, murmuring to himself or lost in some abstraction. How well can we recall the pause before the window when the knotty point cleared itself, and he threw back his head, to gaze with intense returning eye upon the hills that showed between his much-loved trees!

John's school companions (now Professor Calderwood, the Rev. Dr Williamson, Mr Craig) saw at this time, when boys as a rule are anything rather than poet-students, the strong attraction of nature upon him, and how he was drawn to Wordsworth, or any poet in whom he recognised the same love as his own. But mingled with this he had a bright elastic spirit — enjoyment of merry doings, of boyish escapade, and of anything that savoured of adventure.

Often in after-years he would exclaim with

half-humorous regret, that next to the life of a soldier, he would have desired that of an explorer, especially in the far North. Almost a craving for it seemed to come over him at times, when reading of Arctic expeditions, or gazing at pictures of high snows. It had a double fascination for him, — he delighted in travel, adjusting his mind more readily to fresh scenes than to new people; but still more, he was enthralled by the sense of mystery, of cold magnificence, of the un-recorded land, which only the most daring could face.

Here we trace the influence of his own country. Nothing more impressive can well be conceived than the southern uplands of Scotland seen at mid-winter under sunlit snow. On this his imagination might well thrive, as year by year he beheld, with ripening appre-ciation, the subtle outlines, the incomparable curves and slopes, which winter snows bring out in statuesque loveliness. What to the common eye is an almost fatiguing monotony, a country without crest or peak, gave to him at every season a satisfying joy.

That joy was in embryo in the old school-

B

days, and, like other boys, he got into mischief,
was punished for setting on fire the whins on
Venlaw, where he and his companions were
roasting surreptitious potatoes, and heavily
rebuked for harmless proceedings of a roguish
kind in the High Street of Peebles. He had
no nervousness or sense of fear, either when
action was required of him or at his head-work
in school. Examinations suited his cool ready
wit, and in them he always showed well. But
there ran in his nature, and did so all his life,
a curious vein of superstition. The world of
the so-called supernatural, which one could
neither credit nor deny, he saw no reason to
denounce. And something within him responded to the romantic spirit of his own
country, which teems with stories of alluring
kinds,—tales of second-sight, of visions of
beautiful women ; traditions of curse and
revenge and treachery ; centuries of family
feud.

His natural eloquence and sympathetic power
in telling stories, such as that of the ghostly
lady of Neidpath, many a time held spellbound
a group of white-cheeked listeners. But the
feelings of pity, awe, horror, which he could

so easily awake, were in reality his own. He would laugh, and relapse into reserve as the tale ended and the nervous silence was broken by question and exclamation; but those who watched his face might have seen it blanch at his own recital, his eye alight and flashing from within. In his best days nothing could surpass his manner and power in this respect.

In less measure it seems to have been his from almost childhood. He was credulous of the awful and mysterious. Hearing a strange whirring sound in a tree at night, he was filled with thrilling sensations. He persuaded a schoolmate to come next night and listen for himself. The proverbial courage of two discovered a wheel which the wind kept going to frighten birds from a garden near, and disenchantment followed. Full moon broke through the woods, and as the boys walked home, the one noted, and recorded long afterwards, how the other "stood entranced," not wondering at the ancient worship of anything so fair.

John was marked out by his natural qualities as easily first at lessons among his childish

companions. Yet with them he evidently was
on most friendly terms. He did not only originate those essays which in school filled the
other boys with wonder and admiration ; it was
he who out of school started a society which
he called "Socias Manus," by way of promot-
ing good - fellowship among themselves. He
drew up rules which have doubtless long ceased
to exist, although their freemasonry may still
find some echo among those living who joined
in the friendly effort. He often spoke in later
times of his boyish relish for the companionship
of those kindred spirits who cared most, with
himself, to wander the heights and burns, to
dare imaginary terrors, and brave the secret
woods and awful gamekeepers, for the right
kind of "shinty" sticks for school.

It is a quaint picture that we glean from
various accounts by these school-fellows of the
bare, uncompromising old grammar-school. No
partitions within ; "pews" for the classes, well
scarred by hardy penknives ; one map and a
globe, one master and his single assistant.
The boys used to watch for Mr Sloan as he
made his way from house to school, clad in a
certain familiar red-checked cloak. By his ex-

pression of face they anticipated what manner
of master they were to have each morning!
But by all accounts he commanded his little flock
admirably ; and, boy-like, they gave him generous credit for his true character, and very likely
felt it was one to influence and even inspire.
Certain it is that John Veitch, with probably
many another, owed to Mr Sloan a very real
debt for his thorough teaching. Whatever the
worth of his system, the master would tolerate
no slurring, and could detect at a glance the
honest worker from the drone. The value of
this became clear when the terrible examination-day arrived, the event of the school year.
We owe to the Rev. Dr Williamson an account
of it. "Dux" boys were all known before the
examination began. The trial went on from
ten in the morning till four in the afternoon.
All that time a "few ministers" came and went
between the junior and senior schools; "and
the mode of procedure was on this wise. A
Latin class, for instance, was called up. A
book of Virgil's 'Æneid' was professed. Some
one present, known to be qualified, was asked
to select any passage he chose. This was read
and construed by the boys, and questions were

popped at them by all who were able to take part in the examination. . . . The teacher abandoned the work for the most part into the hands of others, unless he had to announce to the examiners that they were not bringing out all that was in a given boy's head." There is an odd humour in this last touch. But we can well believe that it was a "serious business" indeed, to be heckled by the members of the presbytery (or " others ") in presence of parents, friends, and the whole school.

Another diverting incident is given by Dr Williamson, who writes, " It was always matter of congratulation to the senior classes when Mr Elliot, the parish minister, got into controversy with Mr Wallace, the priest of Traquair House, on a Roman personage ! " Bliss for the senior class ! They were ignored, forgotten, while the argument continued.

Under this system John Veitch progressed, "never failing to carry off a load of prizes," and "impressing the examiners with the truth that he understood what he spoke about." " Many of them, I know," adds Dr Williamson, "predicted a brilliant future for him."

The work of the examination-day was for

many years wound up by refreshment offered
to the presbytery and strangers, in the form
of a dinner given by the magistrates of the
burgh in the historic Tontine, High Street.
"And when Mr Russell succeeded in bringing
out distinguished men from Edinburgh, then
was the feast of reason and the flow of wit."
The names of these distinguished persons are
unrecorded, but the day was matter of interest
to the whole town, and as the prize-winners
went home they were often waylaid and their
books and medals inspected with kindly com-
pliment. "Ye're a clever chiel," and "Ye'll
be a Professor *some* day," was often said as
John Veitch's rewards were carefully scrutin-
ised; and one can picture his "shining
morning face"!

Of course such schooling meant many things
left out. Singing, music of any kind, other
arts and sciences, now familiar in elementary
form to every board-school child, were utterly
unknown at the old grammar - school. Not
even such aptitude as John may have had
was given any chance of cultivation, yet no
one could have wished for him that hydra-
headed alternative, the board-school.

In after-years he made spasmodic attempts
to appreciate instrument and song, but it was
easily seen that for him only the emotional
had any attraction. The words of a song
were interpreters to its music. He could not
divine Beethoven, although Wagner touched
him on his dramatic side. But it was merely
a stirring, and fell short of understanding. He
liked to have it explained to him—a thing not
readily tolerated by the genuine musical mind.

His indifference to games points, perhaps,
to another untrained faculty. Manipulation
plagued him ; a parcel done up by his hand
had an unmistakable eccentricity ; his very
writing, though rapid, was done with stiff
wrist and spluttering ink, the table trembling
under his laborious pen ! The foot, which in
its day could do a pattern "jack-a-tar" as
well as any other boy in the place, had a
plant of its own. It took the ground with
great energy, grip, and enjoyment. He was
recognised from afar in a London street by
this alone. No wonder ; his step was so
characteristic, and so amusingly foreign to
what he himself called, with kindly scorn,
" those Piccadilly boots " ! It was expressive

BIGGIE'S KNOWE

not only of himself, but also of the hills which teach the herds their steady swing, and of rocky burn-heads that force the angler to the firmest foothold.

Many an incident arises in memory as we think of the shapely hand and its quick grasp; of the strength, tenacity, tenderness, enthusiasm which seemed to emanate from the whole man, body and soul. And we are helped to imagine the little lad as he reached home at Biggiesknowe, prizes under arm, answering to the temperate joy of his parents, who, "without exhibiting any exaltation, felt very proud of him." "So were we all," adds the generous memory of Dr Williamson. But honours and medals did not unduly uplift the successful boy; rather they proved an incentive and "increased his determination."

Biggiesknowe (really Bighouse - Knowe) is the early home, and there John was born on the 24th of October 1829. The house stands on the slope of green which runs down to the natural margin of Eddlestone Water, where, now a belated and mill-impoverished stream, it passes by the Old Town of Peebles, on its way to unite with the Tweed.

Recent changes and encroachments have practically effaced the twofold cottage, but in his day, and for long after, it was simple and old - fashioned enough. Bedecked with greenery, its cramped windows looked out on the strip of leafy garden and the once clear stream. An apple - tree which blossomed right into the window where John slept, is cut down ; but then it served not only for delight to the eye, but as a means of secret escape to the hills when summer dawns broke, and a boy-ally made with a pebble the recognised signal at the window. That window is small and square, opening inwards, and set rather high in the wall. Within is the narrow room once especially his, its second window looking lowly out on a strip of flowers, and above them the worn iron rail over whose smooth curve John, as a little fellow, went headlong and broke his leg. With characteristic enjoyment in overcoming difficulties, he took to the fiddle during this tedious convalescence, a performance indicating not musical tendencies, but sheer exasperation! Little more can be said than that we can still stand within the rooms, six in all, which saw him from the day of his birth to the close of his college career. One of his parents, or both, found means to buy the house, which eventually came into his own hands. He and his wife went back to it, visitors to the old mother, and again to attend her death-bed; but while his life opened up in other directions, his thoughts often drew him to the past; and not many years ago he asked a friend to make the sketch here given of it, fearing for it the invading hand of time. Like many another, but more ardently than might have been expected, John Veitch looked back on this home. He felt about it with tenderness, and that kind of reverence which gathers about the scene of our childhood.

In one poem ("Spring : a Reminiscence") he speaks of "days . . . that rise in holy light upon the memory" :—

> "O well do I recall
> The first fresh feelings of the heart that filled
> At sight of crocus and the snowdrop fair
> On sunny bank that slop'd to the clear stream.
> And how, a wond'ring child, I stood subdued
> By the new beauty which I would not harm,
> Feeling it sacred as the life of God.
> And now on looking back, Nothing stands out
> In a long lapse of time, save that green bank

Whereon the circles of the years were told
By the return of those sweet lowly flowers." [1]

"You are quite right," he says in a letter to Alexander Nicolson, "in supposing that I have no weak shrinking from men knowing the humbleness of my home. Why should I have such? My own position, as one who has received a liberal education, is a mark of the worth and intelligence of my parents, in that they are thus shown, with all their disadvantages, to have perceived the desirableness of an education superior to their own; and to have possessed the resolution and self-denial needed in their circumstances, to let me have it. I have a pride in them, and trust I shall never be weak enough to forego it."—*May* 31, 1852.

In the same letter, at the age of twenty-three, he is already making passionate reference to the past, pouring out his heart to his friend with that mixture of abandonment and common - sense which is so like him. It is written from the Highlands, to him a form of banishment. "Many a long, long summer day have I spent among the woods of that old

[1] Hillside Rhymes, p. 8.

tower [Neidpath Castle] and beside its ruins; and many an hour have I spent dreaming beside these crystal waters that sweep so beautifully past it. You really struck a chord which has vibrated for a week when you mentioned old Neidpath. The name set me to think over years daily, alas! receding in the past, and called up pleasant memories of boyhood's time, and made me long for another glimpse of the sweet spot.

> " Of dreams that waved before the half-shut eye,
> And of gay castles in the clouds that passed
> For ever flushing round a summer sky."

I must drop this, else you will think me afflicted with home - sickness, or some such femininism. I really am *purified*, however, for recalling my days of innocence, and enthusiasm, and pure happiness, through having its origin in sources so simple."

He could hardly have better expressed the charm that worked in after-years.

PART II.

STUDENT LIFE

STUDENT LIFE.

——————

IT was at an auspicious moment, at the opening of a remarkable decade, that John Veitch entered on University experience. He was just sixteen, and fresh from the old grammar-school, of which, while missing much that it could not give, he seemed to have made the most. The year was 1845.

No record remains of how it was decided, but to Edinburgh he went, in spite of the opinion current in Peebles, that his going was "a wheen nonsense, for the lad should ha' been put to a trede." A compact was made between his parents and himself, and, like many another son in kindred circumstances, he was destined by them, and considered himself from the first

c

destined, for the ministry of the Free Church of Scotland.

His mother went to see John start in the Edinburgh coach; and, knowing the weight of her threat, gave him warning, " Now, John, see ye behave yerself, or ye'll no' get back ! " Not to be allowed to return to college would have proved punishment indeed.   He used to say with a quiet smile, that after-events led him to suppose he " *had* behaved himself." But, for the reassurance and joy of his parents, he lost no time in taking a bursary, and when the letter came with that news, his mother hurried with it to the post - office, that the neighbours might share her pride.   It was no easy matter for such as she to send a boy to college.   Apart from the need of money, which was met by self-denial in the old people and conscientiousness in the son, there existed none of the facilities to which recent times are fallen heir.   To get to Edinburgh there were full twenty miles to walk, while coach and carrier plied on certain days of the week. But old Mrs Veitch did it on foot more than once, and many a time the young student tramped the Edinburgh road, as the session opened or the summer vacation sent him home. That divided life, half the year in the stirring capital and each long summer in the quiet country, was undoubtedly a boon to him, and had a marked influence on his development. For the times were indeed stirring, and, to the raw country lad, not without thrill and wonder. Two years had barely passed since the Disruption, and his mother, who, he said, "allowed him no mind of his own," had brought him up in the Free Church, and dedicated him thereto. Naturally he followed the movement in Edinburgh with all the closeness of an adherent.

By the illiberal rules which then prevailed, Free Church students were discounted, and Free Church professors turned out not only from divinity chairs, but from others besides, Sir David Brewster as well as Dr Chalmers. The result was that a New College sprang into existence, providing extra-mural classes, and, with the emphasis of a fresh enterprise, infusing great vitality into its work. In fact, from the time Veitch matriculated (1845) till Sir William Hamilton's death, ten years after, academic Edinburgh with its Uni-

versity, and its protesting College on the
Mound, passed through a brilliant and fruit-
ful period. "The Edinburgh rhetoric class-
room in the forties and fifties might," says
Mr Skelton in his 'Table - Talk of Shirley,'
"have been a school of the sophists." And
again : "The fame of Edinburgh as a school
of metaphysic and the belles lettres was then
[1850] at its zenith; and to Sir William
Hamilton, 'Christopher North,' and William
Edmondstoune Aytoun, the University mainly
owed its more than European distinction. At
all events, Wilson, Hamilton, and Aytoun were
the three most potent personalities of our
college life." Undeniably this was so, and
every student of the time in Edinburgh hastens
to bear witness to it. But Hamilton, un-
bounded as his influence was over the few
who in his class gave themselves to study,
did not do everything. Among an earlier
group of students of philosophy whom he had
helped to mould, were the late Principal Cairns
and Emeritus Professor Campbell Fraser. And
the latter, along with Professor Patrick Macdougall and others, were the men who, ex-
cluded from any university chair until tests

were in after - years abolished, taught and lectured from the New College.

Thus it came about that, after taking Latin and Greek at the University in his first year, Veitch in his second joined, immediately on their formation, the moral philosophy and logic classes under Professors Macdougall and Fraser respectively. This was at the time a usual method for divinity students. The Arts course prescribed for them preparatory to their theological work was as follows : first year, Greek in the University or under the Rev. John Miller, who held the Classical Tutorship in the New College; Logic and Mental Philosophy in their second year under Mr Fraser ; Moral Philosophy from Mr Patrick Macdougall in the third year; and in the fourth, Natural Philosophy under Mr Forbes, afterwards principal in St Andrews University.

John Veitch began on these lines, but finally went through the complete Arts curriculum of the University, giving himself five years to do it. It seems as if Sir William Hamilton had been as fortunate in finding himself among a fine class of students as they were favoured who sat at his feet. Yet, says Mr Taylor

Innes, one of the most cultured prizemen of a younger set than Veitch, "we were all conscious that he [Hamilton] was not at that time forming any school, and that, strange to say, the centre of youthful and philosophic enthusiasm in Edinburgh was elsewhere. It was to be found in the students who clustered in the Free Church College round Professor Fraser, then in the glow of his speculative youth."

As for the genial influence of Mr Macdougall, it is evident, from the students' letters, that there was no man for whom they worked more willingly. Brimming with humour, and holding his men by the affection he inspired, he was at the same time the firm and careful teacher, and one who sustained a high standard. So that we gather that it was not so much one man, or one class-room, that kindled the enthusiasm of the time, as a happy coincidence, a high average, the blending of power alike in teachers and taught.

And among many drawn together by the common interest, it is pleasant to pause here over the first meeting of John Veitch with Professor Fraser, pleasant to recall the long and intimate friendship which was then born.

Forty-six years after, on the first day of 1892, the Professor writes with the greetings of the season, adding, "This day finds you almost my oldest friend. . . . I well remember how your face charmed me when I first saw it in December 1846." "I saw him," he repeats, now the friend is gone, "for the first time . . . when he entered an elementary class of Mental Philosophy, which I inaugurated on the day of his entrance. . . . I remember the bright and manly intelligence daily reflected in his face, the intrepidity and enthusiasm with which he addressed himself to intellectual questions, increasing with each month, and the powerful individuality which made him one of mark among ninety young men. I recall, too, the affectionate admiration with which, even then, he so deeply inspired me. . . . My interest in him had been so much awakened by the intercourse of that winter, that in the summer of 1847 I made my way to Peebles, on purpose to see him in his early home. I was taken there by my friend Welsh of Mossfennan, with whom I was staying. It was then that I first saw Peebles, a region since associated with so many happy memories.

I have still a vivid picture of young Veitch as on that day, . . . the modest kindness of his greeting, and the interest of sanguine expectation with which even then one contemplated his career."

To some at this time he seemed merely the very grave student, grave with an almost forbidding severity, and suggestive of " Nemo me impune lacessit"; yet whose flights of madcap spirits were astonishing and unaccountable. But not far from the surface there was more to see; and as we gaze now on the faint embrowned photograph of the young man, among other young men, the gentle reflective pose, without the sturdy frame of later years, the fine bent head with silken auburn hair, thick in the fashion of the day, the full pure eye with its speculative intensity, are indeed striking. Lines of his own involuntarily recur to memory :—

> ". . . his deep grey eyes
> As pure and lustrous as a maiden's are,
> Yet wearing oft a far, clear, brooding look,
> As seeing things beyond sight's finite sphere." [1]

" I see him now," writes Professor Calderwood,

---

[1] The Tweed, p. 71.

once both schoolmate and fellow-student, " as he was then : a countenance clear and bright in expression ; the manner quiet ; and the slight stoop from the shoulder, induced by his habit of keeping his eyes fixed on the ground as he came thinking along the street. . . . He entered the classroom with a resolute expression, and made his way with firm tread to the back-bench, far up the room."

Having taken Fraser's and Macdougall's courses at the New College, and carried everything before him there, Veitch went on to the University, whither his reputation had preceded him, and at the beginning of the session 1848-49 he entered Sir William Hamilton's class. It was during this winter that another lifelong friendship began, and Alexander Nicolson and he sat together in the old classroom, where their names are writ up in gold ; or spent happy evenings, and sat far into night discussing everything under the sun, in the "Snuggery," as they called it, of 10 Warriston Crescent. From this time we have a constant stream of letters passing between the young men during each summer,—letters continued over many years, and on both sides

carefully preserved.   Indeed there was inter-
mittent correspondence right on till the death
of Sheriff Nicolson, and we well recall the
sorrowful abstracted expression on Mr Veitch's
face as one evening, fresh from the burial of
his friend, he was living again the old days
which these letters reveal.   Dated   from
Peebles, April 1841, the first begins :—

"MY DEAR NICOLSON,—I have several
reasons for writing to you so soon, and all
of them generically different. . . . Prelim-
inaries over, what I wish you to do for me is
this.   You know Sir William Hamilton, and,
moreover, you intend reading for honours,
logical and metaphysical.   I do not know
Sir William Hamilton, and I intend reading
for honours.   Now, would you go to the
'Illustrious Man' and ask him for his 'Advice
to Students,' which is a printed paper containing an articulate statement of the books
which must be read with a view to honours?"

To which Nicolson two days after makes
reply :—

MY DEAR VEITCH,—I was happy to receive
yours. . . . But I am not pleased at the

manner in which you absconded without letting me have another sight of your metaphysical phiz, or know your whereabouts during the last days of your stay in or about town. (I may remark by the way that such speedy departure was a violation of the Law of Continuity.) However, . . . I have not delayed to do what you requested, but called this day on the Glory of Scotland, the result of which . . . is as follows : . . . 1$^{st.}$ The illustrious man himself has none [of the printed statements], but, 2$^{d.}$ gave orally all the necessary information. . . . B. 1. for the 2$^{d.}$ class of honours any number of modern works in Philosophy, to be selected by the candidate.

"*Cor.* You choose what ones you like ; 'the Selection itself,' *ipse dixit*, 'will indicate the merits of the student.'

"*Lemma.* The number given in is nothing compared to thorough mastery of what *is* given in. 'Accuracy is a good thing. One book well read is better than six nominally,' *sic*. H.

"2$^{d.}$ For the 1$^{st.}$ class of honours some work, or works, in Ancient Philosophy must be given in. . . . Of course 'Lux Graiæ gentis' will be the favourite.

" 3^{d.} He recommended the 'Chronological order' in the study of the works. . . . I hope the above will satisfy you. . . . Of course it *must* do so, for you can get nothing more."

Breaking away from these business-like remarks, he exclaims : " What a villain you are to choose that subject for writing on ! I will not attempt it ; that of course is a corollary to your proposition. Shall you do No. 1 also ? I think I must even try a whack at Brown, an ungrateful task, as the poor fellow gets smashed by everybody. . . . I have done nothing systematic yet, but shall begin to peg into the Greek and Latin as soon as the things are published. I must, however, make Natural Philosophy my great concern, though it's a horrible affair. As for Algebra, it's only fit for heathens and Saracens."

This last opinion the friends shared, for neither mind lent itself in the least to mathematical matters. Both were at this time teaching at odd hours, in order to make money enough for college expenses, another bond of mutual interest. Thus the above letter goes on : " I began my delightful task of teaching . . . the

Roman tongue yesterday. . . . The lady is a tall, good-looking, black-eyed Puseyite of about sixteen *ætat*. I must be on my guard. . . . I must coat my heart with *robur triplex*, three-fold Presbyterian blue, to resist the dangerous influence ! . . . Write soon, a more creditable effort than your first, which was just an interrogatory and two preliminary apologetic sentences, and believe me, yours affectionately, ALEXANDER NICOLSON."

After a few days the following leaves Peebles, its paper close covered with a free, strong handwriting, words dashed here and there, and the straight lines flying as they near the end :—

"MY DEAR NICOLSON,—I was happy to receive your 'smasher' of date some days ago. I am grateful, to a certain degree, for the information communicated. Seeing, however, that gratitude is decidedly a duty of *indeterminate* obligation, and in my opinion one of these which it is both convenient and expedient to *reverse*, I promise you an equivalent 'whacking,' in kind and degree, about the Assembly time. You ought (case of Associa-

tion) to 'whack' that chap Brown : you could
do the fellow in two nights ! As for Edwards,
I hope (what presumption !) to send him the
way of all the dead. (You must see that a
dead man after being '*ignored*' is killed a
second time.) I think Edwards must have
been a sort of good fellow, but somewhat
lean. If he does not become Jonathan Edwards *Redivivus* it won't be my fault, as I hope
to give him sixty hostile pages. . . . Most
certainly the Glory of France, the fellow who
has again intellectually united Scotland to
her old political ally, deserves consideration,
and he shall have it. . . . I intend likewise to review Sewell. . . . I don't intend to
enter into any lengthened or articulate criticism of the principal vulnerable, yet hostile,
momenta that fill your last. . . . As for the
law of continuity, that was not violated, unless
remaining in town ten days longer than were
necessary was a breach of it—and if so, the
law itself is a *misnomer*.

"I have to address a society here to-night
. . . on capital punishments."

This society was probably the " Peebles Literary Association," which Veitch is believed to

have founded, and of which he certainly continued a member for years. Its meetings were
held in a tiny dark room, the vestry of the
Free Church at Peebles, which went by the
odd misnomer, "The Hall." Criticism and
debate went on, essays were written, and,
says the Rev. Dr Williamson, himself a
member, Veitch's papers and speeches were
always replete with originality, and were
listened to with great attention.

"I have to address a society here to-night
on capital punishments. I am the second
speaker; ergo, I have no speech ready. . . .
It is, however, probable I may *dress* the fellow
who opens, and thus kill two dogs without a
bone. By the way, how are you getting on
with these horrid Ethics? I am not reading
. . . any of it at present. But the seventh
book is a bit of a bore. It may be, however,
that the difficulty arises from my plunging
in medias res without any 'preliminary apologetic sentences.' . . . I think I shall read
'Aristotelis de Anima' for W. H., which, with
Berkeley, Locke, Leibnitz, Cousin, &c., &c.,
will make a pretty decent appearance, though
not a *phenomenon* by any means. I must

secure some of the Schoolmen on it.   It is
quite impossible to read it *proprio vigore.*
Do you know how much reading there might
be in the three volumes of the 'Organon'?
I should like to get it up likewise.   You may
have all my essays from Macdougall when that
worthy gentleman has completed his *peroratum,*
which I hope will be ere long.   Take care of
the highly lauded Puseyite.   It strikes me
she is making an impression. . . . A woman
and a Puseyite, being two evils added, equals
a horrid evil in all."

Letters hasten to and fro at this time, parcels,
papers, books, coming and going between the
students, and full details of the work each had
on hand fill the eager pages.   It is the student
life of that decade at its best.   Veitch, the
session ended, went on studying at home in
Biggiesknowe ; and owed a debt, which he en-
thusiastically realised, to the friend in Edinburgh, who spared no pains to procure books,
and to see them safely in care of the carrier
who plied twice a-week between the old burgh
town and the capital.   Anxiously awaited,
always acknowledged, these books had also to

be paid for. And we find Nicolson in charge of a small sum, which refunded him for occasional purchases and the cost of carriage. He questions how to deal with a certain precious note-book, "unless it might be safe to send it open at the ends, for which the postage is only 6d."; and packages with many seals would reach the "Snuggery," the summer essays come from Peebles, ready for delivery into the hands of the professors "favoured by Mr Nicolson."

The letters become steeped in the very vocabulary of metaphysics; and that personal influence so markedly attributed to Sir William Hamilton shows both consciously and unawares in the close merry pages, where "H." and "*sic* H." recur frequently after remembered phrases of the teacher; and such expressions as the "Glory of Scotland," the "Dictator in Metaphysics," the "Great Man," and the "Great Master" testify to the faith Sir William inspired, and the charm which held his students. For example, Veitch writes, "Since the Dictator in Metaphysic, &c., has homologated what to me seemed sufficiently dark, I am prepared to *swear* to the truth of the thing."

Phrases in Latin, Greek, and French occur

D

often in these epistles, but German was still formidable to Veitch in '49. "By the by," he writes, about that Trendelenburg [he had asked Nicolson to procure it], "I am not aware whether the book is in German, High Dutch, or Broad Scotch. In fact I never saw it. . . . If it be in German, it shall rest in peace for me ; . . . I will none of him ! . . . If Trendelenburg is in an unknown tongue, I shall use my discretion as to which of Aristotle's Logical, Psychological, or Metaphysical Treatises I will hereafter peruse. It will be the shortest, of course, for *very little* of that gentleman is long enough to me, with so much on hand." After giving some absurd details about getting an old hat done up for a shilling, and testing it in a shower of rain with disastrous effect, he says, " The only consolation . . . is that it *was*, and of course *is*, only my *second* best, which I am prepared to demonstrate syllogistically is as good as the Rev. Dr B–ch–n–n's premier, though he — *i.e.*, the man, not the hat — has been pronounced the 'Prince of Preachers.' In sooth Dr B. may be thankful that his great mental powers, which are not so very great after all, lie lower, and therefore

in a stranger case,—than his hat!" This Dr
Buchanan was Professor of Theology in the New
College, and was the well-known author of a
book entitled 'The Work of the Holy Spirit.'

If a letter begins in exuberant fun, and
few are without fun, it will suddenly fall
into a serious key, telling of the absorbing
work, which, to Veitch at any rate, was un-
feignedly a delight. We can picture him
rising betimes all through the summer at
Peebles, and resisting the appeal of "grain"
and "hope," to sit in the narrow room where
the desk, and strewn papers, and sofa covered
with books, marked his isolation, and yet
favoured his reflective habits. Into a special
box in his own separate door the postman
dropt those many letters, no doubt marvel-
ling the while.

We must not, however, suppose that he was
lonely or unsociable. "He became," writes the
Rev. Dr Williamson, now his fellow-student,
"a frequent very welcome visitor in my mother's
house." He was fond of fun, enjoyed summer
expeditions, and the balmy evenings boating
up Tweed to Neidpath, and the friends took
many walks together. At these times of re-

laxation he was like a boy set loose from
school. But it was ever with open eye, and
with genial talk, and the ready passage from
Wordsworth or other poet. Dr Williamson
was not only familiar with the old house at
Biggiesknowe; he knew the work going on
there, and even—at a later date—copied out
for Veitch while the Life of Dugald Stewart
was in process; and there they laughed together over the printer's mistakes in decipher-
ing the writing of John.

But study was not so easily carried on, nor
material so simply to be had, in these still
not distant times; witness the following quotation from Veitch: "I am truly obliged to you
[Nicolson] for the pains and trouble you have
been at in getting these notes. I wish you
would send them entire. The mode of sending
them will be this. When you go to Castle
Street at 4 o'clock P.M. you can go by Princes
Street, from the end of which — *i.e.*, at the
Register Office—the Peebles coach starts. . . .
Give them to the coachman addressed to me."

During this summer his work was, " For
Macdougall I intend writing, as I said before,
on 'The Will,' Scottish Natural Theology, and

perhaps Sewell, and reading Leibnitz and Butler. As to the Ethics, I am not sure : if nobody is going to read them, I will, for the credit of the class. Indeed I think I will at any rate." Cousin, and Locke, and Trendelenburg's ' Aristotle' he also had on hand, and in his letters we feel the powerful leaven at work within him.

The near prospect of finishing his course, and thereafter devoting his life to the Church, forced upon him questions essentially interesting to him then and always, for he had all a Scotchman's leaning to Theology. After six pages of fun and teasing he bursts out on page 7 : " I cannot but think it a stain on our Churches, and men in them, to have acquiesced so long and so unthinkingly in the doctrine of Necessitation, or rather of a necessitated volition. I know that this arises from their holding ' Election' views. These I hold too; but we ought not on that account to annihilate the notions of merit and demerit, or at least render them ridiculous. I think I shall manage," he naïvely adds, " to be perfectly orthodox, though for that, of course, I do not care a fig, provided it had not been the true, or what seemed to

me the true. However, I think there is a
great deal of rubbish which requires clearance
connected with what is termed Calvinism. Indeed there is no treatise, so far as I know,
where the doctrine is put upon its real and
only valid footing. Edwards" (on whom he
was writing at this moment for Macdougall,
"56 pages and no prospect of a terminus")
"has a good many valuable things in it, but is,
to any one that will push things a few inches
beyond their *status quo*, thoroughly atheistic."

From passing remarks of like nature, crude
though they may be, we gather the drift of
his inner life. And every now and again the
chafing against the confinement, the longing
for a different freedom from this so dearly
bought, flashes out. Nicolson was in his Highlands during this summer, and wrote ecstat-
ically of sun-burning and idleness. It was a
very hot summer from May onwards, and John
Veitch from his small room, rising with daily
headache, and sitting for weeks at a time till
two in the morning at work, often heads his
epistles "very hot," &c. "How I do envy your
position *ad interim!* . . . I am not sure . . .
that it is the pure and disinterested love of

the sublime with which I am actuated. . . . I hate the Stoics with a perfect hatred, and am somewhat of an Epicurean. By the way, from the sublime to cream" (on which Nicolson had dilated), "and from cream to Quintus Curtius, and from this latter to the classical part of the M.A. examination, do you think I will be able to do the Greek and Latin during September and October, devoting the whole time to them? I mean to do it thoroughly, annotating it."

Presently we find him in the thick of this classical reading, but as October opens he begins to modify his scheme of work. "I have just finished Edwards (in word and *thing!*). Scottish Natural Theology stands at this moment at 44° below zero. Half-a-dozen pages more, I expect, will sink the *concern!*" This calls forth from his friend an amusing caution. "Commend me to you," he writes, "for bearding the lion in his den; you are quite up to that sort of thing! And you have swamped poor Scottish Natural Theology in a sea of *Critik der reinen Vernunft*, logic, and technology. Let it go then, if, as is to be feared, it is only a well-meaning but unseaworthy log, with no stable Higher Metaphysic keel to bear it up. Only, I do hope you will put something better in its place." Having on the appointed day despatched the two essays, one on the said Natural Theology and the other on "Pleasure and Pain," Veitch goes on to tell his friend what he intended to do in winter. "I suppose you are living in the belief that I am going to make this my fourth session by taking Forbes. Such is not my intention. I have resolved upon making my course extend over five years, and accordingly will take Wilson and Sir William, for which—*i.e.*, the Logic—I will work, attempt its daily exhibitions, &c. . . . I am labouring away at the Greek, expect to finish the Philoctetes to-morrow, and Æschines in great part this week. After that I must steal a day to visit the Rev. William Welsh of Broughton. . . . I have not wholly lost hope of Sir William's essay [on the Will]. . . . Were I writing for him I would make an effort to come near a finished affair historically and critically, the former of which I despair of doing ∵ of my absence from books. The latter I think I could manage *tolerably*."

Mr Nicolson, himself an able student, and

endowed with fine literary sense, was unsparingly critical of the country student, and yet generously shows what he expects of him. At this point—the winter of '49-'50—they fall out of each other's course, Veitch going forward to a fifth year. "I am doing my best," says Nicolson, "to make Utilitarianism look as black and blue as possible. . . . I have come quite to the other pole in morals since last winter. I am now in danger of running into the extravagance of making happiness appear nothing, when before I made it everything." Then he goes on: "You must decidedly, if you attend Wilson this winter, throw your whole soul into a refutation of his doctrine, which really leads to bad consequences. Of course you are to be Primus in both Logic and Moral Philosophy. Nothing short of that will content me, or be worthy of yourself."

So the beginning of the winter session found Veitch again sitting at the feet of the "Dictator," and of "Kit North." No doubt he took Hamilton's class a second time simply because he enjoyed it. It seems that this was common enough among the students. Dr A.

B. Bruce, for example, who entered Fraser's class with Veitch in 1846, tells how, his love being Mathematics, he took it three years consecutively.

The "apathy and contempt" with which the best men then regarded the Edinburgh Arts degree is well known. It was granted in some subjects without examination and after a few minutes' conversation, and was hardly taken, or asked for, save by schoolmasters or those for whom it had a superficial value. Few of Veitch's friends thought of taking it. The restraints of a strictly prescribed curriculum being thus slackened, there was freedom for the individual, now unknown. Consequently his special taste and bias were fostered, and we can well imagine that the liberty of choice readily outweighed the fictitious honour evaded. This state of matters was ended with the Universities Commission of 1858, when the degree of Master of Arts was raised to a position of real academic value.

Meantime Sir William Hamilton had been partially stricken by paralysis: "The massive brow and calmly observant eye were clouded, the articulation was defective and laborious, but he struggled bravely on, and the moral effect on the students of that shattered body sustained by an indomitable will was immense." [1] It is an interesting picture that we get of this classroom; of the students' hero with his disabled arm. "As the hour advanced," writes Professor Calderwood, "and the analysis of consciousness went on, the younger fellows, first weary, became restless. At such times Veitch, all attention and quickly wielding his pen, would grow impatient and mutter in displeasure. . . . The Professor, with an earthen jar before him, jostled inside it cards, on each of which was a letter of the alphabet, and drew as chance would have it. Any student under the letter drawn might rise and give an account of the lectures which had been given since the previous oral examination. When V came up, immediately Veitch rose slowly in his place. The event was one of interest to us all : he gave an account of the Professor's reasoning so clear, so full, so appreciative, that it left no doubt that he was . . . first man. His achievements in this way live in the

[1] Table-Talk of Shirley, p. 41.

memory, and they pointed him out at the time
as a thinker of no mean repute."

At the close of the session Veitch carried off,
for the first time in student memory, the
highest honours in Logic and Metaphysics,
and the gold medal in Moral Philosophy.
Even Nicolson had reason to be satisfied, and
the eyes of the younger men followed him
approvingly.   One of these was Mr Taylor
Innes, then in his first year of Philosophy,
but who, a twelvemonth later, repeated
Veitch's feat.   He says, "There was a great
contest who should have the second place,
but no one had any doubt that Veitch was
the first : his calm mastery of every side of
every subject that came up had impressed
us all ;" and "there was universal enthusiasm
over his double honours."

Before this time the students of Professor
Fraser's class — Veitch at their head — had
formed among themselves the Metaphysical
and Ethical Society of the New College. A
society of like name apparently existed before
New College days ; it was, however, scarcely
alive, and could not provide members enough
for office-bearing within it.   But under the

influence of fresh blood the younger society
ousted or absorbed the old, and began to
usurp a unique place in the life of the
University, over which a wave of philosophic
interest seemed to be passing. New College
and University students alike poured themselves vehemently into this Society, and its
diploma of honorary membership, conferred
among rare instances upon Veitch himself,
became much more prized than the despised
Master of Arts. For many years he was an
active member, a principal figure in the
" Metaphysical," until, and indeed after, it
migrated to the University with Professor
Fraser himself.

Friend after friend of these early days
gives evidence as to the influence which, by
hidden ways, gradually asserted itself, and it
was acknowledged without grudge that Veitch
became *facile princeps* among men with whom
it was honour to be young. " They looked
up to him," says Professor Knight, then himself a student in the University, " much in
the way that the young *élèves* at the college
of La Flêche looked up to the boy-philosopher
Descartes, who soon left them to found the

Modern Philosophy of Europe. . . . He was one — and by far the most original — of a brilliant group of students."

John Downes, Alexander Nicolson, James M'Gregor, Alexander Bruce, John Wilson, Andrew Wilson, Gavin Carlyle, John Stevenson, William Knight, George Wilson—all of Veitch's year, or thrown together during the greater part of their course—those were some of the comrades of this time, not a few of whom, with Veitch among them, are gone into the silence. Their plain student names, like his, thus baldly read, convey no impression. But, with hardly an exception, they all became men worth knowing — scholars and *littérateurs*, men of thought, of action, of truth. It was a happy chance that gave Veitch the sympathy and stimulus of such fellow-workers, and the place they granted him among themselves was no doubt the most encouraging fact of his life at the time.

" The divining instinct," continues Professor Knight, " of the Scottish student, was perhaps as finely developed, and as keenly exercised, in its diagnosis of merit at that time, as ever before or after ; and this came out, not only in the way in which the best essayist was appraised, when he read his papers in the classroom, but also, and even especially, in the verdict passed upon his work in the Debating Societies."

Besides the "Metaphysical and Ethical," there were the "Dialectic," the "Diagnostic," and the "Exegetical," of which last "classical scholars who intended to become clergymen were members." Mr Knight did not join that Society, but was attracted by the signature on the notice-board, "J. V., secretary," and went to one of its meetings. Essay and essayist are forgotten, but, he adds, "I remember well the keen eye and clear speech of the Secretary; his firm incisive manner, and the way in which, young as he was, he guided the whole work of the Society. . . .

"But it was mainly in the 'Metaphysical and Ethical' that Veitch's powers as an undergraduate came out. Every student interested in Philosophy joined that Society; and he usually felt that he owed more to the essays read and discussions there carried on, than to any other academical influence, excepting the personality of Hamilton." Veitch was "the chief—the representative member—in those delightful ever-to-be-remembered years."

Mr Taylor Innes, referring to Veitch's influence in the "Metaphysical," says : "He maintained his connection with the Society even after he had joined Hamilton's class and had gained its honours, and we who had been only at Sir William's rather grudged this assumption of superiority. But the first night on which we were admitted as guests to the 'Metaphysical' changed our view. The essayist that evening was George Wilson, afterwards Mr Veitch's brother-in-law, and I remember to this day the revelation he made to us of what could be done in the way of concentration, and almost consecration, of the mind for speculative ends. It was in him a permanent possession and attainment, and to the end of his life, amid all the roughnesses and pressure of business occupation, there shone out in him that which attracted us so early : not refinement of mind only, but an inward crystallisation of soul. There were other able men present ; but Veitch rose above them all. He was generally in the chair, and had the duty of summing up the discussion. I have often since heard that duty performed by celebrated men, but never with such absolute success as it was in those days by him. Without notes and without preparation, he gathered together all the parts of a long and complex discussion, presenting each in its due proportion and in its relation to the rest, and unfolding the result with a weight, wisdom, and power quite unequalled in my experience."

Thus, as he gained an assured footing among his fellows, there began to gather round him friends such as only a man of character can hold, in spite of differences of upbringing, and the usual conventions of acquaintance. Work began to come to him, as presently we shall see. Then, after 1850, he entered certain theological classes of the Free Church, by way of carrying out the original dream both of his parents and of himself. These, however, were soon dropped: not that they lost favour with him, for he "retained the keenest interest in religious questions, and would trenchantly discuss them to the end of his days." But, as Professor Fraser says, " the ecclesiastical atmosphere was uncongenial, and finally helped to determine his strong bent to philosophical

E

liberty." That there was more complex reason for what seemed to some his defection, is clear from his letters to his friend Nicolson. And there can be little doubt that his critical habit of mind, combined with a passionate and deeply religious nature, played curious havoc for him among the teachings and dogmatising of the time. But this, and it would seem the whole content of these transitional years, is laid bare in the correspondence here presently continued.

The spring of 1850 shows many advances, greater maturity and intensity in the young student, now twenty - one. A day or two after coaching to Peebles, the winter's work over, we find Veitch writing to congratulate Nicolson on his B.A., and awaiting the arrival of his own prize-books from Hamilton's class-room. "You are the first," writes Nicolson, "to give me on paper my new title, this day solemnly conferred by the time-dishonoured, rubbish-compiling hands of Professor ——."

"I congratulate you," says Veitch, "on your Bachelorhood, . . . and may you never stain it . . . by any synthesis whose elements you have not fully sifted."

There followed on the prize-taking and close work of the session some weeks of reaction, which are easily imagined. The friends seem to change places, and that natural indolence which is said to have told against the Celtic Nicolson all his life fell upon Veitch, the usually unflinching worker. "For me," he writes, "I am joined to my idols. Can you . . . at all realise the position of one who is sunk in the lowest depths of indolence, who sleeps some nine hours per night, and does nought during the livelong day? I positively am of opinion that I shall never be able to withstand the current which has set in upon me."

From the first he was specially attracted by Descartes, and Professor Fraser had long before this "suggested a translated edition of the 'Méthode' as work that might some day be congenial to him." But now the translation, just begun, is thrown aside, and he cannot bring himself to resume it. "I am too lazy to move." So he betakes himself to other reading, a refreshing draught from other wells.

' I have fallen in . . . these days . . . with

Shelley. . . . To the highest metaphysical acumen he unites one of the very finest imaginations. Such a union makes one despair, and almost objurgate their lot. He is blasphemous enough. . . . I have always heard the poor man branded with all the terms which theologic hate can coin, and I know that the knowledge of what is bad in the fellow is widespread. But with all his blasphemy and denunciation of Deity and Christianity, I immensely prefer him to all the whining evangelicals I ever heard or read of. Nay, I subscribe to every word of Shelley, where he denounces *what he observed was mistaken for* Deity and Christianity; though, poor fellow, he was himself mistaken in thinking that such was all,—and the truth. Shelley is the only man who fairly represents my conviction on the doctrine of necessity; though, *i.e.*, he gives the whole of what I believe sufficient to supersede the doctrine as commonly held, but not what is necessary to save the dreadful consequences of the dogma. He is a consistent Necessitarian. Thus sings he :—

> 'Throughout those infinite orbs of mingling light,
> Of which our Earth is one, is wide diffused

A spirit of activity and life,
That knows no term, cessation, or decay,
That fades not when the lamp of earthly life,
Extinguished in the dampness of the grave,
Awhile there slumbers; . . .
But active, steadfast, and eternal, still
Guides the fierce whirlwind, in the tempest roars,
Cheers in the day, breathes in the balmy groves,
Strengthens in health, and poisons in disease.'

Again :—

'Spirit of Nature! all-sufficing Power,
Necessity! thou Mother of the world,
Unlike the God of human error, thou
Requir'st no prayers and praises.'

These extracts are from his 'Queen Mab,'
the unrivalled work of a youth of eighteen!
Strange to say, Shelley is also an idealist.
This dogma he clothed in imperishable verse.
Everything that is, but seems and 'is a
vision' :—

'Thought is its cradle and its grave not less,
The future and the past are idle shadows
Of thought's eternal flight; they have no Being;
Nought is but that it feels itself to be.'"

It must be remembered that these are
merely a young man's impressions on the first
reading of the poet. We have to submit to
the choice, not from the finest of Shelley, but

rather to that in him which answered to the best in the student. It is a question whether Veitch ever enjoyed Shelley the poet, as he seized upon Shelley the metaphysician. Yet the "imperishable verse" made its own impression, and without doubt gave to his receptive mind fresh literary impulse and a new standard of excellence.

Most men and women look back to a time when Shelley absorbed them, and threw his fascination over their very thoughts; and John Veitch was no exception. But he never in after-life quoted Shelley, though much of that singing might well lend itself to the lover of Nature; and one is fain to conclude that with the passage of these fervid years when Veitch was as emotional, passionate, impressionable as young man could be, the poetic thirst allayed, Shelley in great measure ceased for him, partly because there was sterner grist to be ground, and partly because deeper affections and the supreme mastery of Wordsworth were yet in store.

The interlude, which included idleness and poetry, had a grave and solid reaction. He is absorbed once more in the abstract. So much is this so, that Nicolson teases him about it, and is almost fatigued by it. " I have just received your acceptable *essay*, shall I call it ? Very much 'Letters - to - a - German - Princess' style, even more profound." Still, the sympathy which each counts upon is never lacking ; and in the same letter, after pages of clever fun and serious sayings, he bursts out, " Give me an Infinity of Perfection and an Eternity to work in, and I'll solve you anything." The attempt to " solve . . . anything" did not vex the soul of Nicolson as it did Veitch, yet the former was intellectually the real sceptic of the two.

Presently we find Nicolson, aware perhaps of the danger in his own temperament, which Veitch can hardly credit in any one, saying : " I suspect I am fully more idle than you after all, . . . as far as regular persistent study is concerned. . . . I am at present doing nothing but attending the Assembly, writing letters, and reading Macaulay's History. That word *persistent* puts me in mind of an ode or hymn which, if you have not heard before, is worth your hearing. As you give me Shelley, I will give you Goethe. It is translated by

Carlyle in his 'Past and Present,' a book which
I earnestly recommend you to read, for pleasure and profit.   Here is the song :—

> 'The mason's ways
> Are a type of existence,
> And his Persistence
> Is as the Days are
> Of men in this world.
>
> The Future hides in it
> Good hap and sorrow.
> We press still thorow,
> Nought that abides in it
> Daunting us,—onward. . . .
>
> And solemn before us
> Veiled the dark Portal,
> Goal of all mortal ;
> Stars silent o'er us,
> Graves under us, silent.
>
> But heard are the Voices,
> Voice of the Sages.
> The worlds and the ages
> Choose well—your choice is
> Brief, and yet—endless.
>
> Here Eyes do regard you
> In eternity's stillness ;
> Here is all Fulness,
> Ye brave, to reward you,
> Work, and despair not !'

"I think that is . . . sublime : it stirs my

spirit in quite an unspeakable manner. I have not read Shelley, but shall do so. That idea of Necessity as the Supreme Power is grand and solemnly true, but dreadful and uncheering, if you have nothing more ; in fact, ' *requiring no prayer or praise*' makes it a thing, not a Person, . . . an inconceivable, if not a nonsensical, idea. I am astonished at a Poet, and one, I believe, of extraordinary sensibility, giving utterance to such a cold sentiment. I have more sympathy, however, I confess, with such a belief rationally adopted and sincerely acted on, than with the ' blear-eyed bigotry ' (Dr Duff's words) that shrieks its condemnation without knowing anything about it, but that it differs from itself. Positively it moves my scorn to see people, themselves immeasurably short of the high standard even of heathen morality, presumptuously sitting self-chosen Cerberi at the gates of Immortality, and taking upon them to say who shall or shall not enter in."

These and like extracts may not touch us now as in themselves weighty or original, but do they not bring out some of the influences of the time, and within the narrower sphere of the young men's lives, which made of both robust and able men of letters, men who cared for the best things, and books, and people, and whose hearts burned within them for righteousness' sake?

Close upon Nicolson's degree came the announcement which drew indignant exclamation from Veitch. Nicolson saw it, and with his love of the incongruous, and of teasing a friend who had no great sense of humour, though a great fund of high spirits, he quoted in mocking capitals, "Are you aware you are down in the Advertiser of the 'North British Review,' and that in company with Dr Thomas Chalmers?

> 'III. Translation of Descartes on Method. By John Veitch. [*In the Press.*]
>
> 'IV. Prelections on Butler, Paley, &c. By Thomas Chalmers, D.D., LL.D., &c.'

The thing is atrocious. To put down a lie, '*in the press,*' is bad enough, but to put it . . ." thus "is too bad." To which Veitch replied with matter-of-fact vehemence: "That advertisement is a shocking affair,—shocking from its falsehood, and from the impertinent juxtaposition of a little and a great. I am endeavouring after a stoicism in matters of authorship, and hope to be able soon to look on aught of adverse, as upon aught of favouring decision, as somewhat which exists, but affects not the merits or demerits of a production. . . . This resolution is, however, premature."

Still, the 'Translation of Descartes on Method' was a first essay, and was due for publication in that summer of 1850, and we can imagine it cost him no small pains, and was met by the usual criticism, however kindly.

Presently he begins to write for books again. "It will save expense and trouble if you . . . put these together as soon as procurable, . . . and call at 100 Grassmarket for Aitchison, Peebles carrier." Besides the translating, he was still of a mind to take his degree the following winter, for the work's sake, not the diploma. "Next year," says Nicolson, "I expect to see, Logic 60—Veitch 60 ; Metaphysic 110—Veitch 109 ; both 170—Veitch 169 !" And again, "May you prosper in your 'Method' : see that you give us a good *stunning* introduction."

A week later, and a third of the translation is done, ready for his friend's perusal. Fourteen days to finish it, and "then comes the tug of war, the introduction." In characteristic parenthesis he complains of a certain French paper as "an exceedingly mystical, if not nonsensical, affair. Flay these Frenchmen! there is nothing like good Scotch thinking yet!" This sentiment did not, of course, stand wear. In after-years he would often express his admiration for French philosophical writing, the exquisite definition and exactitude of terms.

By the middle of June he fell ill, and after the attack of bronchitis was over, there was a daily "swimming sensation in the forehead," solely from "not having seen the green fields for ten or twelve days." Still he resisted his friend's invitation to spend three weeks in "my own Celestial Land of the Nibelungen" (Skye). "I could not, however," answers Veitch, "think it other than gross sacrilege thus to lose twenty-one days from the summer. . . . I must be up and doing." And in the autumn (1850) his first effort was published. As we shall see, it

was followed in '53 by his translation of
the 'Meditations' and of selections from the
'Principia' of Descartes. "In this way,"
says Professor Fraser, "Veitch has the credit
of introducing the French philosopher to the
English-reading world."

It is perhaps not without interest to hear
what the young man has to say on this very
matter of translating; and indeed the whole
letter has a freshness and frank nobility,
which is sufficient apology for its nine long
pages :—

"MY DEAR NICOLSON,— . . . I am
greatly obliged to you for the efforts put
forth on behalf of my interests. . . . I
have since received the part of the 'Method'
from MacDougall. . . . He says in his
note, 'My wish was . . . to give here
and there a touch of greater ease, perhaps,
and freedom — so that, if possible, the very
thought of its being a translation might disappear.' Hence you perceive his impression
. . . that it is not free enough in some
places." (Nicolson had criticised it as too
free.) "I intend to act on this, . . .

though with such an old writer as Descartes, it is hardly possible. At the same
time, I protest scrupulously against alter-
ing or polishing the sense for the sake
of greater ease and freedom. . . . I suppose, however, that owing to the rapturous
frame of your soul in the meanwhile" (Nicolson is in the Highlands), "nothing that relates to the darker sciences, or their authors,
will have much interest for you. . . .
Living among, and hourly conversing with,
the beautiful, &c., one is apt to entertain
. . . infinite scorn towards the meaner
realities of life. . . . By the way, the
notion of the beautiful has suggested to my
mind a topic of interest, I mean [Dr] Duff's
eloquence." (On this subject Nicolson had
just written with enthusiasm.) "I have
read with care some of his best orations,
and therefrom experienced high gratification.
There certainly burns within him, and that
intensely, a noble fire; an enthusiasm com-
mensurate, if this is possible, with his position as a Missionary of the Cross, who is
really and truly nothing short of a Herald
of the Absolute. At the same time, . . .

I don't rate highly even the highest imaginative power, when not kept in strict sub-
ordination to the ends of the purely speculative intellect. I don't object to imaginative
energy being realised for its own sake and
to accomplish its own ends. Legitimately
you cannot have an act of imagination out
of relation to the end of the faculty. But
this end itself ought to be subordinate to
other and higher faculties. Above all, people
ought never for one moment to be left to
imagine that the stimulation of their emotions
(æsthetical) is a very lofty employment, or
better, *passion*, and that thus the end of
their existence will be more thoroughly realised. The truth is, I cannot help regarding
such men as Duff as somewhat unfortunately
placed when, with their high powers, they
have to make application of these to the
extraction of a few tears from young men
and maidens, and sprigs of theology generally; and in sooth, I suspect that the . . .
majority of the frequenters of the Assembly
—*yourself* always excepted, with of course
many others — are like the frequenters of
the theatre, there simply for excitement,

being a more respectable . . . [rabble], but
still a rabble. That savours perhaps of something akin to presumption, but it contains a
sound spice of truth, and is quite the impression of the 'impartial spectator.'

"I enjoyed a perfect treat the other morning. I had the honour, sir, to breakfast with
the Rev. John Cairns of Berwick, and the
greater honour of a prolonged colloquy with
the second Sir William (not second-rate, mark)
of Scotland. I found him quite to my taste;
a very child in simplicity of manner, and a
very giant in profundity of intellect. He is,
however, no ape of Hamilton, but objects,
and I think solidly, to several points in the
philosophy of that 'illustrious man.' Strange
to say, he has the same objection to the fun-
damental point in the Metaphysic which I,
unaided by any previous hint (pardon me
the egotism), elaborated in one of my recent
summer essays. I suspect, really, that Sir
William is wrong, and if so the highest
metaphysical problem (this Cairns allowed)
must be given up as insoluble. Then! it
ill becomes us to boast of the speculative
intellect; for this tells us either of our de-

ception or our impotence. Perhaps Kant was right, and, in deducing or holding an Absolute Cause or an external entity, we are objectifying illegitimately the merely personal laws of our being. If so, we are in a life

> ' Where nothing is, but all things seem,
> And we the shadows of the dream.'

At least Kant's alternative and Sir William's exhaust the whole possible.

"By the way, I must communicate to you, as my friend and confidant, a resolution which for some weeks has been in a state of formation. I intend, as soon as free of the ' Method,' to commence inquiries in the field of Natural Theology. These I shall throw into a regular treatise, . . . and present in 1854 to the Competition of Theologians. In the event of failure,—at which I would not for a moment be surprised, . . . and would not take sorely to heart,—I may find means of making it see the light. The investigation will be the means of at least permanently settling my own convictions."

Presently, as August passes, he says : "In good sooth I can acquit myself neither of illness nor laziness. I have been suffering from . . .

headache.   Lazy I am always from constitution and inclination; in truth I am heartily
ashamed of my summer's work. . . . I confess
I don't regret much the little I have done. . . .
I have grown tolerably stout,—indeed look, I
believe, rather like a coachman!"   It is somewhat diverting to us who know how closely he
worked in these and other days, to come across
his reiterated conviction that he was "lazy—
always."   "Early rising," he writes in a letter
penned before breakfast, "in a man of my
lymphatic tendencies has an important moral
influence; for just in proportion to the difficulty with which it is accomplished, in that
proportion does the fact of my 'erectness out
of the mechanism of Nature' the more sen-
sibly appear."   Again, when Professor Fraser
commended his dilatoriness with Descartes'
'Meditations,' setting it down to "notions
of perfection," Veitch exclaims to Nicolson,
"Good soul! it is sheer idleness!"

The summer of 1851 found the friends more
widely parted,—Veitch acting tutor to the son
of Mr Brodie at Lethen House, Nairn; and
Nicolson in London, overwhelmed with the
weariness and expense of sight-seeing, but

filled with amazement over the first International Exhibition and the Crystal Palace. To us, nauseated with exhibitions, his comments are amusing : " It is, in fact, a glorious vision, the nearest thing to the showing of all the kingdoms of the world, and the glory of them, in a moment of time, and assuredly a strong temptation to fall down and worship."

The Queen was visiting this wonder daily, in the early morning, and study within it was part of the education of princes of all nationalities. At the same time young Kingsley was drawing crowds, and vexing by heretical eloquence the soul of Puseyite London. One sermon on "the Church's message to the working classes " turned out to be " the working classes' message to the Church, and created an extraordinary sensation." Kingsley was openly rebuked in church, but the people rose and followed him on leaving it !

Elsewhere Father Gavazzi was electrifying even hearers ignorant of Italian ; and to Nicolson he seemed "the only truly Demosthenic man I have ever seen, . . . such grace and power and variety in his delivery, that to one who understands his words, it must be perfectly irresistible.   He is a tall dignified figure, and with his long robe flung over his shoulder . . . looks the most classical thing you can imagine."

And of course the young Scotsman must needs visit the Houses of Parliament and record his impressions.   These are not favourable.   "The first view of the Senate gives anything but a dignified impression," he says; and after a great deal of quizzing at their expense, he finds that their oratory pleases him no better than their apparel.   "Can it be," he exclaims, as a certain noble lord gets upon his feet, "that you are the ablest statesman in this great empire!"

And as a corrective to all this pomp and frivolity and emotion, there sat in Chelsea the prophet Thomas Carlyle; visible—audible! Of course Nicolson counted him among the sights of London, and went.   "There was," he relates, "another gentleman, . . . so I had not such an opportunity as I wished of hearing him [Carlyle] speak on particular points, but his talk is most glorious."   We can imagine with what interest the young devotee of the

Free Church read what follows : " He touched
a little on the state of the Churches, and the
' difficulty or impossibility to young men of
ingenuous minds to commit themselves to any
of the *crazy old machines.*' In fact, if they
had ability or energy, it was worse; for they
' set themselves to *plaster up all the old
falsehoods, thereby constituting themselves more
solemn and tremendous impostors under the
moon*'! Fancy that! He spoke with great
admiration of Dr Chalmers, 'a man of great
veracity, a man who had a *great quantity of
fine speech* in him; a large amount of quiet
energy; and a fine large humanity' ('not,'
he said, 'soup-kitchen humanity, but I mean
in the right sense of the word'). Then he
said, with emphasis, that he (Chalmers) was
the 'only man of genius of this age who
followed Theology.' He speaks in a deliberate
racy manner, with a thoroughly Doric utterance, which is refreshing to hear, and his
laugh is most hearty. He has a noble face,
somewhat shaggy hair . . . with a sprinkling
of grey, . . . deep beautiful eyes, good nose,
. . . and a lower lip of immense firmness
and satire. There is no restraint in his pre-

sence. You forget the stern denunciating prophet in the genial homely man."

Meantime in the fresh North, and far removed from his usual surroundings, Veitch was settled to his work as tutor, and tasting for the first time the pleasant novelty of country-house life. After undergoing a "most painful sea-sickness," for he travelled to Nairn by boat, he finds his new position "exceedingly pleasant," and is almost surprised by the "very kind" attitude which Mr Brodie's household adopt towards him.

Three or four hours daily were devoted to his pupil, and the rest were his own. So, with his usual enjoyment, he set about learning the new country, its features, history, and interests. He first tastes the sea from the rising ground opposite Lethen House, where in a magnificent view eight counties met.

It makes us smile now to note the silence with which Veitch in his retreat greeted the outpourings of the sight-seer Nicolson, who, on the rack of London at the hottest of the season, was longing, but for the impossible expense, to clothe himself "like an Armenian or Persian, for coolness' sake"! And when the reckless fellow finds himself "without money to pay the week's rent," three pounds are despatched, not without difficulty, from the far North, and received with shouts of thanksgiving! "But," adds Nicolson, "as you are living in such clover, you can stand that. Really you have a famous berth. . . . I should like to pay you a visit!"

Meanwhile the work of translating Descartes' 'Meditations' was proceeding, and the selections from the 'Principia' were also under way; and in spite of Carlyle — perhaps the more because of him — Veitch intended "beginning immediately a regular and sustained course in Natural Theology."

From his "Den" at Warriston Crescent Nicolson presently writes once more, harking back, it is true, to the "Syren city," yet well content to be home. He gives a highly absurd account of his eight-shilling sea-voyage from London to Granton, as involuntary deck-passenger amidst a dense crowd of visitors returning from the Exhibition; among whom "everything was obliged to give way for the one absorbing idea." It took from Wednesday night at 9·30 till half-past six on Friday

evening ; still, what between woolsacks for a
bed, a ringdove cooing in the cabin, and a
couple of books (Terence and Horace) from
the enticing London bookstalls, Nicolson got
sleep enough, and rejoiced the more over the
"deep Sabbatic calm" which reigned in de-
serted Edinburgh on his arrival. It is now
Veitch's turn to be sarcastic. "One thing is
clear," he writes, "from your exordium, that
the air of these two nights has not cooled
your imaginative sentiments. The exordium
would itself almost sell a three-volumed novel.
I predicted—mentally—from the mere perusal
of it that you had been to the *Adelphi*—or
to *Carlyle!*" But quickly passing from this,
he takes up other themes, describing the
country about Lethen, and fixing with his
vivid historic sense on the "one spot of deep
and thrilling interest, Culloden Moor. . . . I
think you are aware of my Jacobitish leanings ;
you will not therefore be surprised when I
tell you that I looked upon it as a piece of
holy ground—holy in the best sense of the
term — worthy of reverence. . . . No one
whose feelings are awake, and seek their
proper objects, can fail to be affected by the

mere contemplation of sincere (even while erroneous) purpose, when the reality of this has been sealed and attested by the blood of him who entertained it and sought its realisation. . . . I was secretly thankful, however, that the battle was one day in '45, and not a particular Saturday in 1851, as, with all my chivalry, I don't imagine it would have carried me to the point of submitting to the tender mercies of . . . the commander of his Majesty's troops."

This little confession is in reality witness to something constitutional. For at no time in his life could he endure the notion of bloodshed; he would blanch at the commonest accident, and turn away from a cut finger. He could not understand any one in the miseries of illness, and was, apparently, more impatient of the distress than sympathetic with the sufferer. The imaginative horror which thrilled through him had instant physical effect. Going through a *salon* of many years ago, in which pictures of carnage and frightful details predominated, he passed with a set face from room to room, compelling himself to note what he had come to see. But

it soon became intolerable, and with a kind
of fierce sorrow he cried out, "Awful, most
awful! this is the very scum of the national
thought!"

This intensity of realisation came into play
at every point in his experience. At the
theatre, which he enjoyed with something of
the once-theologian's sense of stolen delight,
he would be completely carried away by the
story, the scenery, a character, a voice, and
remain unconscious of all else to an extent
hardly credible. But the faculty made him a
unique companion, whether in travel or at
home. He did not fatigue one with petty
things, never hurried along by common routes,
nor attempted to see the customary sights
because they were customary. But, taking
in fresh impressions with boyish, often merry
pleasure, he bent his mind to its habit of
grasping the real nature and interest of what
lay about him, without oppression and without
tedium.

Travel, however, was not to be counted
among Veitch's experiences for yet many a
day; and we have to turn back to glean from
the letters how matters were going with him.

The old subject ever cropping up excites Nicolson to say: "It does strike me that a good masterly sweeping away of the rubbish that pretends to be demonstration, once and for ever, would be a service to English Literature, Theology, and common - sense, even though nothing further should come of it, and . . . I do consider that to this service you are specially called." Needless to say the gigantic task remained in limbo as far as Veitch was concerned.

It gives us an idea of how closely the young students sailed to the wind in money matters, that presently Veitch found himself in need of five shillings, from having lent so much as three pounds to Nicolson in London! Promptly the latter posted a pound-note to Nairn, with the feeling words, "There is nothing so horrible as being in want of money in a strange place." This want made itself felt on a larger scale and without regard to locality, as the autumn went on, and in September Veitch wrote that he would not return to Edinburgh in the winter. "It is a hard thing for Rhetoricians and speculative men generally," he says, "to be obliged to condescend to the con-

templation of the relation between pence
and potatoes; yet such a speculation . . .
involves considerable difficulties. The adage,
'Money is the root of all evil,' has a peculiar
exemplification in my own case, since it is the
proximate cause of my exile." The resolve
was not made without sacrifices, of which he
makes light. "And so," groans Nicolson, "you
are not coming this winter. . . . I have
no doubt you will be far better where you are,
and can work more uninterruptedly." But
"whom can I take up with me unceremoni-
ously into my 'Den' to help me to solve the
'Sphinx riddle,' and freely canvass 'things
new and old'? No doubt I have good
fellows. . . . But for the man that can
not only discuss but define; wade in the
shallows and swim in the depths; . . . in
fine, that can see through formulas, and hit
the mean between fear and presumption;
limitation and licence; bondage and anarchy,
—for him I must wait!"

To which Veitch sends a warmer, if less
effusive, reply: "I had intended to say something by way of sentiment, seeing that I am
to be exiled for a winter from the city of my

alma-mater and choice companions ; and thee, *amice*, with whom my companionship has been by far the sweetest. After your last, however, I am somewhat afraid to venture on the 'depths.' . . . That 'Snuggery,' sir, is a consecrated place, sacred at once to the Muses and Metaphysics, to Mirth and Meditation, the Sportful and the Speculative. There is something . . . in the atmosphere of it that elicits the latent scepticism of the understanding, ay, and *creates* it where it did not exist. It is comfortable to have a place where one can lay aside a long Sabbatarian face, and without danger of being mistaken . . . freely canvass the things that are held in repute. . . .

"From all the help yielded by the meetings in the 'Den' to this healthy scepticism I am shut out here, . . . forced wholly to refrain from such topics lest I should do hurt, and . . . be myself misunderstood. *Sed verbum sat sapientibus.*"

By this time Descartes' 'Meditations' were announced in preparation, and Nicolson begins a busy winter, teaching added to his usual work, — for, he says, "I must make money somehow."

Whenever the 'Meditations' were out of hand we find Veitch sending for books, buying books, sadly in need of "Hume, the subtle Doubter," and reading generally in earnest. "I am now only beginning to work my way from Metaphysics to Theology; my progress is very slow, but probably as rapid as it ought to be." After a curious letter dealing with the nature of sin, he alights upon Newman with sudden and characteristic fire. "Ere men come to see eye to eye, they must be satisfied to trust less to reasoning and more to intuition and feeling, or whatever name you use to designate that which, not being reasoning, is yet above it; less to the logic of human nature and more to its spontaneous development — its *poetry*, if you will. But hold! that is rather too much. I advise you, don't trust greatly to men like Newman, whose inner texture is certainly fine, but whose logical part is of the slip - shod style. I don't quite sympathise with, or approve of, that method which, while it professes to overthrow its opponent's dogmas by reasoning, at the same time denies that its own are to be tried by a similar standard."

Thackeray's "new serials" were at this time coming out, and Veitch mischievously recommends them, along with Dickens, as excellent fare during certain "dry-as-dustic" lectures of a teacher who shall be nameless. He had recently bought Coleridge, by the way, and was slowly widening his literary horizon.

As the year's correspondence closes, he explains his refusal to go to Edinburgh to enrol for a "partial session" by a consideration quite beside the expense of journey and fees. "Of course it would save a year, but I want to be ready to *preach* in three or four years —if ever."

Nicolson was at this time "laden with work" : besides five hours' duty at the Advocates' Library, and his evening teaching, he was Extraordinary Assistant to the Professor of Rhetoric and Belles Lettres, and was helping Principal Lee in reading the Moral Philosophy essays ; all the while studying theology, and, by the help of Carlyle, arriving at certain decisions, negative but distinct. "That same Confession [the Westminster] it is but too evident I never can before God and man, with a free soul, swear to as mine. . . .

I would equally turn Manichæan or Fire-
worshipper, and of course, it likewise followeth
that I can never be a minister of the Free
Church; and all but equally certain, of none
other. Such is the lamentable . . . conclusion.
The future is as blank and doubtful as can be."

Having "astounded the fellows in the Theological Association by uttering 'damnable
heresy' on the subject of original sin," Nicolson draws down on his own head a common-
sense rebuke. "So you have been coming out
in the 'Theological.' Be cautious, however, how
you do it. Don't tilt against received prejudices unnecessarily; especially avoid attack-
ing them in their received terminology (as
the doctrine of this or that). A fellow, by
becoming a heretic too soon, loses what influence he may otherwise possess. . . . Nevertheless," adds Veitch, "keep hammering at
the fellows." Alluding to the "Metaphysical,"
he says, "That Society, sir, will send some
fresh blood into our Church, and it has much
need of it. . . . They have lately made
me an honorary member."

The result of the said "hammering," and of
making a vaguely heterodox impression all

round, was, that Nicolson was called up by Professor Cunningham, and his opinions kindly but vainly questioned, "without," as he himself has it, "much result"! With much humour and vehemence the scene is recorded in full, and ends: "To think that because a man, fronted at once with the whole array of theological dogmas, takes upon him to examine and question them, he is therefore to be marked as an unwholesome entangled sceptic, needing the help of learned Professors, to take him by the hand and guide him into truth, is really the quintessence of imbecility, and everything that is servile and degrading." He longs for Veitch, that the little explosion might have "resulted in something more open and alarming"! But though the incident is fast forgotten, it seems to mark a change which has been coming, and which we now feel *is come;* and after the following utterances, we realise that Veitch, like Nicolson, will never enter any Church as "Herald of the Absolute." "I can't for the life of me see that a man in this [Nicolson's] state [seeking his way to a rational and manly acquiescence in the dogmas of the theological standards] is a heretic, or

G

any nearer heresy than he is to orthodoxy.
Nor can such a condition be a ground for alarm
to any one the most scrupulous. In point of
fact, in performing this process you are merely
discharging your duty, — as he who never
went through such an ordeal . . . as certainly omitted doing what he ought. To
seek to extinguish this spirit of inquiry, for
the satisfaction of oneself (if such be the
aim of the New College dignitaries), is as
hopeless as to essay to turn the sun from its
course. Besides, where would be the Protestantism they profess if such a thing were
carried out? where civil and religious
liberty? Truly this is liberty from which I
would fain be free, and Protestantism against
which I protest. . . . Were the entrance
into the Church more generally made in this
way — were the theological dogmas accepted
because ascertained to be true by each individual — there would be more tolerance in
our churchmen, and less of unchristian bigotry
and sickening cant. There would be more
tolerance toward others, because there would
be some experience of doubts and difficulties
on the part of the believers of the dogmas.

"And I for one am resolved that, though I am stranded on the shore of heresy, I shall never attempt to maintain any theological doctrine which I have not for myself thoroughly sifted and found to be true. 'He who *will not* reason,' says the author of the Academical Questions, 'is a bigot; he who *cannot*, is a fool; he who *dare not*, is a slave!'"

In this spirit he carried out his own investigations to their issue, upholding his like-minded friend. And this, although he was never stranded among heretics, and probably went through no crisis more serious than belonged to every thoughtful student brought up as he had been.

Let us realise, however, the integrity and moral courage with which the two friends threw aside not only their advantage, but what seemed the only career open to them; for no couple of Covenanters could have been stauncher for silent conscience' sake.

Whatever may be thought of Veitch's wisdom in giving his life to philosophy, there can be no doubt in the mind of any one intimate with him, that he did well both for himself and the ministry of the Free Church

in going his own way. Even if he could have
joined it conscience clear, there was that in
him which could brook no compromise, and
his power of presenting sympathy to his fellows
was limited, even feeble—fatal hindrances in
dealing with the souls of men. He would
either have become a combative and purely
missionary preacher, strong and eloquent no
doubt; or he would have sunk into the lax-
ness which is the curse of defeated energy.

There are some who believe that in taking
to philosophy he defrauded us of the fruits of
a fine historic sense. He had a great hanker-
ing, often expressed, for historical work. "The
true history of Scotland," he would exclaim in
regret, "has never been written! If one only
were a dozen years younger!" And a col-
league of his own once said, "Had he chosen,
Veitch could have given us a finer History
of Mediæval Philosophy than any man of
his day."

But it is sufficient to remember what philosophy did for him, how the study was meat
and drink to him, and what a lost mind he
would have been without it, to reconcile us
to possibly imaginary losses, and to lay less

stress upon what *he* did for philosophy, without withdrawing honest recognition and admiration of his service.

"We must try," wrote at this time his friend and fellow - student, George Wilson, "to subordinate circumstances to the purposes of our higher life, and beware of subjecting ourselves to these circumstances :—

> ' Still to be strenuous for the bright reward,
> And in the soul admit of no decay.' "

The thought finds echo in Veitch's words (to Nicolson), "Really a man has to make exertions for a living in this world, of which those whose circumstances are different truly know nothing. It is good, however, I find, to be so tried and circumstanced. . . . I really would not be happy had I nothing to fight and struggle for ; and I don't care much though this should be my lot through life, if it be made to conduce to the refined gratifications of intellect and moral feeling. Why, man, it is but a few years at best. . . . And there is something within one in the shape of an . . . ambition to do somewhat for his race and time, however little, which of itself is a great encouragement in the struggle for a livelihood."

In May of 1852 the question came up of his return or not to Lethen for the next winter; "to be settled with myself in a few days. . . . I am quite at sea. Were I resolved for the Church, I should have no difficulty,—but there—there—lies the knot." Nicolson is in the same straits. "I have to . . . fix deliberately what I am to *do*, whether to turn east, west, south? (Northward there is nothing to be got!) Staying here is the plain of destruction; . . . a man must have a work."

Meanwhile "Christopher North" retired, and, after times exciting to the students, and interesting to all, Professor MacDougall was "duly inducted by the Town Council, the Senatus refusing to acknowledge their right to do so. The point had been pending, and now a crisis was come, and Sir William Hamilton's academic wrath waxed fiery over it all." The idea of a grocer having any hand in regulating the domain of metaphysics was to him "supremely disgusting." "However," adds Nicolson, "the grocers don't manage these things so badly after all" (they had just put in the students' favourite)—"better, I suspect, than choleric professors would." Ferrier was the other candidate, the rest having dropped out.

Lethen House left behind, the summer closed in a delightful time of holiday at Peebles. Veitch had, of course, not seen anything to be compared with home since, at this time twelvemonth, he left it; and as soon as Nicolson's foot, cut in bathing, relieves him from reading Dante and quoting Carlyle, they proposed to themselves a tour in the Border country—a tramp with knapsacks.

But so vague are both young men as to the future, that they actually debated the wisdom of quitting their own country for colonial life! "What think you," says Veitch, "of the Diggings, or as you seem meanwhile to be looking in that direction, the Backwoods? Really, if anything turns up in that quarter that would do . . . for *two* (don't mistake me), I should be greatly disposed to join you." So much for the study of philosophy!

As Nicolson and Veitch saw more of each other, and the friendship crystallised, their

letters became fewer, simpler. Yet the post-
script often recalls the first of them : " write
soon," " write, you rascal," " write, and don't
keep me in agony." Still the letters were not
now a daily need, and naturally so. Such
friends could rest assured of each other in all
circumstances ; interests widened, experience
deepened ; new friendships formed. One of
these last concerns us immediately, for it must
have begun about 1853, and it became a sustained and very intimate bond. But, unfortunately, Veitch's letters to George Wilson
have been destroyed, and only from the con-
text of those of the latter can we gather the
inwardness of the tie. They met as under-
graduates, studied together in philosophy and
theology, shared lodgings during a part of that
time, corresponded closely for five or six years,
and finally in 1862 became brothers-in-law.

The influence of this friend was something
quite distinct from that of Alexander Nicolson :
it was salt and salutary, intense but restrained,
with nothing of the exuberant charm of the
younger man and earlier friend.

With a certain sensitiveness, not uncommon
in a man young and self-equipped, Veitch re-

sented any imputation that he cared for money, or indeed for title or honours of recognition, or the very opinion of others. Of course he *did* care for these things quite as much as a sensible man should, and Wilson perceiving the weakness, humorously appreciated the fact. " Act up to your vaunted principles of unconventionality," he writes, with the severe candour of understanding. Again, " I judged you by myself, and I think I am as indifferent to money as you are. But I have always thought you must dislike . . . your present manner of life [tutoring, &c.], . . . both because it is in itself unsettled and precarious, and because it does not *secure* to you the means . . . necessary to independence, and were I in your circumstances I would be tempted by any offer of fixed employment, were it not particularly uncongenial. . . . [Some such offer made to Veitch gave rise to the letter.] Far be it from me to ruffle your magnificence by insinuating that you want money. Nevertheless, you are so far human as to wish to be and to do many things, which without this filthy lucre you can neither be nor do in this world. . . . I did not mean anything inconsistent with your being quite as sublime in this respect as you can possibly imagine yourself."

In reality, the "vaunted principles" were more practised by his friend than ever by Veitch himself, who was then, at all events, too little of a man of the world to allow himself deliberately to toss aside accepted traditions. Indeed he was only acquiring knowledge of them. Yet in reality both were men radically separated from the conventionalities— in the one case by choice, in the other by circumstances. That the one remained, as he gratefully said, "still a private individual," while Veitch from the beginning commanded an audience, does not alter the fact, any more than it could change the regard with which each looked upon the other. But it is certain that Veitch gained both in a worldly and in a spiritual sense from this friendship, what he could nowhere else within his circle acquire; and it is touching to read, after the keen-edged sentences, the friendly smiting and sarcastic hint, an occasional burst of feeling towards him, which seems to alarm its very writer.

It was late in the summer of this year that Veitch set out on his first travels. So absorbed was he in the new scenes and his own impressions, that his letters (to Nicolson) are scant and empty. Indeed the correspondence, as such, lapses. Veitch seems to have kept no more of his friend's epistles, and it is only occasionally that we can glean from his own what was passing between them.

York, Cambridge, Lincoln, London, and the English Lakes made up the little round ; and the contrast between his one letter from London, and the bright effusive pages he received in 1851 from Nicolson when there, is not without interest. What strikes him in "this tremendous city" is that "life indeed appears to me to be quite automatic,—it is all *work*, no thought ! The whole thing, moreover, appears so natural, so spontaneous, that the problem of *when* man took the resolution to do as they are doing—*i.e.*, performed the mental part— seems as difficult of solution as the determination of the period of the origin of the heavens would be from the constant revolution of the stars alone. . . . Withal, there is something . . . sublime in the surpassing amount of energy one sees, or rather, strives to conceive as here displayed. . . . But it is merely the

physical sublime. . . . After all, the thought
of it fails to touch one so deeply . . . as a
single act of moral heroism where the apparent
interest is all on the side of wrong."

On St Paul's his comment is that "its *extensive* grandeur perhaps surpasses its *intensive* beauty," and he turns back in thought to the Minster just seen at York, to the "airiness of the Gothic, with most beautiful harmony amid great variety." But in Westminster Abbey he is beset by the strange sadness which may be felt within those subduing walls. "Nowhere," he exclaims, "such testimony to the omnipotence of death, for there at his feet lie valour, and grandeur, and worth, and beauty, and genius. . . . Verily, the men whom this nation delights to honour have a magnificent repose. . . . Let us keep alive the memory of the great dead—God's too often despised gifts to a faithless generation; for then, reminded by the stars beckoning to us afar, . . . we shall be less apt to forget our destiny and haven." With that his thoughts, as always when deeply stirred, reverted to home and his own country. And in the description of the resting - place of

the Many buried without strife made, and
without honours gained, we recognise the
very spot where his own body now lies, yet
not without his share both of struggle and
of honour. "For such . . . there may be
room in some quiet green graveyard beneath
the shadow of a spreading tree, the wide
heavens for overarching roof, and pillared on
the everlasting hills—where the repose . . .
is certainly not less still."

In the winter and spring of 1844-45 Veitch
once more returned to his boy pupil, and his
letters from Rothesay and other places, where
he stayed with Mr Brodie's household, contain
little beyond jottings of the reading he had on
hand—Scott, Keats, Kingsley, among the rest.
"Being shamefully behind in works of fiction,
I have been reading up . . . of late, that is,
at leisure hours when physical strength did
not avail for anything higher; for I am as
jealous of my energies as any man, and would
as soon commit suicide as sit down to a novel,
poetry—or Kay's Edinburgh Portraits—in the
forenoon." As for places, what "some people"
consider dulness he feels to be a proper degree
of quiet. Perhaps some "unimaginable lodge

for solitary thinkings" was already a reality to
him, quite apart from his own quotation from
Keats.

He was working in the intervals of teaching
at his Life of Dugald Stewart, and was so en-
grossed in one way or another that when winter
sets in he writes, "Beyond barometric notices
there is absolutely no news from this land
[Nairn] of mountain, mist, and snow." A
period of quiescence, of undercurrent, had
set in; there was either too much to tell his
friend, or nothing at all. A quieter spirit per-
vades the letters, and the avoidance of metaphysical matters is evidently conscious and of
purpose.

And then, as sometimes happens, a chance
circumstance arose, which really defined for
him his place and work in the world. He was
just upon his twenty-sixth birthday when a
letter came from Sir William Hamilton, asking
him to assist him in the work of the Logic
class. Keen as Veitch was to accept this, it
threw him into new perplexity; Mr Brodie,
the friend of so many years, was in trouble.
And not even Sir William's tempting offer
could make him leave the house which had so

hospitably entreated him. So in his dilemma he fell back on Nicolson, who, ready to help at any cost, was accepted by Sir William as Veitch's proxy until January 1, 1856, when he freed himself finally from his work as tutor.

He had but short tenure of the office, for Hamilton's days were even then numbered, and in May 1856 he died.

Soon after, Veitch went to visit Professor Fraser at Church Hill, and found such stress of work to do as he had not hitherto known. After promising to Messrs Black, publishers, an essay towards a certain forthcoming volume, he finds it "quite impossible for weeks to come"; adding, to Nicolson, " I don't mean to venture rashly into print, and without counting the cost. . . . I am borne to the ground with work; I have only this day got my hands clear of the 'Review' for November, and already the horizon is darkening with new clouds of emergency." Part of the work that so embarrassed him at this time was the superintending of the 'North British Review,' in which he helped Professor Fraser for a year, when the latter, who edited

the 'North British' then and during the six
preceding years, was under the first pressure
of his new duties at the University. Professor
Fraser, succeeding Sir William Hamilton, had
arduous work before him, and he retained
Veitch, not only to help him with the 'Review,'
but for four years as his assistant in the
University.

"In that summer," says Professor Fraser,
"he stayed with us for some weeks at
Church Hill, endeared to us all." And during
it they went together on a memorable visit
to Yarrow. For at Tibbie Shiel's they met
Campbell Shairp, "afterwards amongst his
truest and noblest friends,"—" to whom," says
Professor Fraser, "I had the pleasure of introducing him." There sprang up from that
beginning another friendship, the mutual sweet-
ness of which was only ended by death—one
which was of peculiar value to Veitch, as
satisfying the very heart and core of him, a
relationship beautiful to see.

Indeed 1856 was a year of good events,
crowned as it was by his engagement to
Miss Wilson, the only sister of his college
friend George Wilson. Of course there fol-

lowed upon it many midnight talks between the young men, and letters more personal than was their wont. "It is true," writes Wilson in reply to an appeal from Veitch, "that there has always been not a little that I felt to be defective both in your views and character. I think . . . I must have made you aware that such was my opinion, although a sense of my great deficiencies and inconsistencies (much greater, I believe, . . . than any I could ever observe in you) has made me feel it too like hypocrisy to refer more explicitly to these defects. I have thought you not only devout and sincere " (this was the matter of discussion), " but growing more devout, more earnest, and more consistent. Unless I had so thought of you, I trust that no affection for you (and perhaps you do not know, and may never know, how deeply and tenderly I have loved you) could ever have induced me to permit your intimacy with one who is dear to me as my own soul." How much this means from one who says of himself, "I have too strong a tendency to 'eat my heart alone'"! It is his parenthesis that speaks—that is repented of

H

in the next letter, but not in after years revoked, in spite of separating experience.

In the following year (1857) Academic reforms were on foot, and came into play in 1858 under the *imprimatur* of a Scottish Universities Commission,—" and it was thought desirable," says Professor Knight, " that one or two of those who had scorned to take the M.A. degree under the old conditions should now receive it *honoris causa*. Few were admitted,—I think only four : John Downes, J. Sime, George Wilson, and John Veitch. Veitch was thus Master of Arts *honoris causa*, and no honour was ever more justly conferred."

When winter came round again the Memoir of Dugald Stewart, which had proved such an arduous task, was published, and Veitch sent a rough copy to Nicolson for review, by way of light reading on a journey, adding : "Dugald, as you know, is but a poor subject for a man of mere speculative capacity to come out in. But I have sought to do justice to his general merits, which I believe to be very great."

Some peculiar difficulties had presented themselves to him in working at this book, and, before it reached final form, he wrote for George Wilson's opinion. "I think," replied the latter, ". . . you ought not to suppress so strong a conviction. . . . You do not speak of Stewart merely as a philosopher or political economist; you give your estimate of him as a man. You hold that he was not a religious man, and that his influence was positively irreligious. You hold, moreover, that there is an entire absence of real godliness in all the best-known Scotchmen of Stewart's time, and that this has blighted both their memory and works. I cannot but think that if you pass this over without remark, you will place your own character in an ambiguous light."

In regular work and the absorption of the new circumstances, 1858 - 59 slip away unrecorded, save in letters of George Wilson, who, referring to their similar plight, writes : "You also are a brother in like adversity. Most strange! that men who *once* seemed as if about to be finally absorbed . . . into the Absolute itself, should become so miserably enslaved to such unmitigated relativity as this! Shall we call it the last infirmity of noble minds?"

Assisting Professor Fraser, whom the young men nicknamed " The Sage," Veitch waited for the close of the session to go off to Auchineden, his *fiancée's* country home, where he was awaited. " What day," writes his impatient friend (George Wilson) in the well - known phraseology, " does the Sage dismiss the gentlemen 'as such'?"

PART III.

AFTER-DAYS

AFTER-DAYS.

THE years were now come which were to put Veitch's matured nature and disciplined mind to the inevitable test. From the time when, at thirty-one, he succeeded Professor Spalding in the Chair of Logic, Rhetoric, and Metaphysics in St Andrews University, we look for the fruits of the life, and we watch the deepening processes which gave concentration to his powers, and at the same time defined his limitations.

The telegram worded "Mr Veitch is duly elected," which left St Andrews on the 30th of May 1860, was a source of rejoicing among Veitch's friends, and of relief and gratification to himself. The anxiety of some months was over, and his future practically secured. He had worked well for it. Besides the annotated version of the works of Descartes, there was the ' Life of Dugald Stewart,'—" a work," wrote Dr John Brown, " so rich in varied knowledge, and in evidence of the widest and most exquisite culture, that no one could think it the work of a young man, unless from its *vis* and freshness." And besides these, he had, as Sir William Hamilton's literary executor, edited, with Dean Mansel of Oxford, the ' Lectures on Metaphysics,' published in 1859, about the same time when Veitch tried for the Chair of Logic in the University of Aberdeen, and lost what Bain got. And now he was engaged in preparing for the press the second volume, namely, ' Lectures on Logic,' from the hand of his deceased master.

Testimonials are proverbially unreliable and absurd, because they describe, and must describe, a man as one would a garden guaranteed to grow no weeds. But three little slips of print remain to us among the scanty records of Veitch's candidature ; and, coming from the hand of three men whose partiality was founded on intimate knowledge of him, and of the truth about him, are worth perusing again. One was Professor Campbell Fraser's ; another came from Alexander Nicolson ; and from Dr John Brown's pen as delightful a tribute to a young man as could be paid, even by one who had " watched his [J. V.'s] progress through life, and through thought, with an interest quite peculiar." Professor Fraser, in forwarding the cause of his assistant and friend, spoke naturally to Veitch's distinction as a student of Logic and Metaphysics, " among the foremost of those who have at any time appeared in the Matriculation Lists of this University." He also referred to Sir William Hamilton's very high regard for Veitch personally, and also for his philosophical knowledge. After rehearsing his literary work, &c., &c., Professor Fraser alluded to the confidence of the students in Veitch's judgment, and their respect for his ability, and their large attendance at his tutorial, but voluntary, classes. " He is one of the ablest academical examiners of whom I have any knowledge."

" His experience in the business of teaching was that which," says Dr John Brown, " of all others best fits a man to inform and quicken as well as to expound,—the Socratic, or examinational method." " Modest, self-contained, genial, energetic, with a deep persistent enthusiasm, authoritative, honest and intrepid, firm and clear in thought and in action, curiously free from the fashionable vices in speculation in thought and in style, of the present day, I know no man," continues the same generous advocate, " more certain to make young men think, and think rightly, and to influence for good their whole after lives, or more certain to enrich and adorn that philosophy of mind which is the growth of our country, and one of our first possessions."

Every one who remembers John Brown knows how he combined with his singular charm and bubbling humour a childlike candour and benign simplicity, which excused every eccentricity, and which, taken with his gifted nature, produced the effect almost of genius. That candour and simplicity give weight to the few sentences in which he virtually summed up the life—especially that part of it which we have now passed—of the young man he knew and liked so well.

"Very early in life," he says, "with that quiet firmness which is one of his master qualities, he took up his line, and perilled everything upon keeping unflinchingly to it. He deliberately, and with the full knowledge of all its dangers and hardships, negative and positive, gave himself up to philosophy proper —to the search after truth in the world of thought—and from this path he has never once swerved. In the noble words of Shaftesbury, ' he has ever held that the true workman abhors every transgression in his art, and would rather starve than act contrary to what he reckons the justness and truth of work.' "

Nicolson, at the time sub-editor of the ' Encyclopædia Britannica,' entered the lists for his old friend by calling especial attention to the spirit in which John Veitch had cultivated philosophy ; and in closing, he touched on the more strictly personal. " A more independent and decisive judgment in philosophical as well as in practical matters, combined with a most cautious and reverent spirit, I do not know. . . . I have found him in all high and manly virtue a man among few, of whom it can be

said, as it was of one of the best and greatest
of Scotchmen, that 'into his breast no ignoble
thought ever achieved an entrance.'"

Thus it came about, on the strength of combined fitness and the favouring moment, that
Veitch went to St Andrews, and began, not
new but independent work. The kind of thing
some of his friends expected of him, without
of course foreseeing academical changes which
must nullify their hopes, may be gathered from
a letter of congratulation from George Wilson
just after the appointment was announced :—

"MY DEAR VEITCH,—Receive my hearty
congratulations on your having got the Chair,
. . . and on what must be hardly less consolation, being out of the horrid ordeal to
which you have been subjected for so many
months. I hope the editorial work is over too.
. . . Be sure and *hold* to the resolution I have
so often heard you express, of not conforming
to the Scotch practice of constant lecturing,
which is a mischievous absurdity, being hurtful
to the minds of the students, and still more
hurtful both to the minds and bodies of the
teachers. It was easy to denounce it in

theory, but it will cost you something in practice, quietly to act contrary to a long-established custom. I cannot help looking to you with some hope that you will do something to put *fresh practical life* into these noble speculative studies."

Thrown now with such men as Ferrier, Tulloch, Shairp, Sellar, and Forbes, it was no wonder that Veitch enjoyed keenly his new circumstances and place; and that, although disliking the sea and seaside places with the inborn narrowness of a mountaineer and a bad sailor, he ever looked back on the four years at St Andrews with affectionate regret, and spoke with a reserved tenderness of the spot where, in 1862, he and his young wife made their earliest home.

It was in the autumn after his appointment that Peebles, observing honour done to her son, woke up to the idea of being in no wise behind-hand. "The Magistrates and Council have resolved," writes Veitch to Nicolson, "to present your humble servant with the freedom of the city of Peebles! . . . and also to give a dinner in the Tontine Hotel at 4 P.M. of the same day. . . . Are you able and disposed to grace the important ceremony? . . . Come, like a good fellow. . . . The whole thing, presentation and dinner, is an awful calamity, but there was no way of getting out of it."

This personal and perhaps eccentric view of the matter was only one-sided, and did not affect in the least his sense of the courtesy and congratulations of his friends. But probably he felt the occasion would try him; hence his entreaty to Nicolson. Professor MacDougall, whom the Provost of Peebles invited, could not free himself to come, but wrote a long, and, to Veitch, most flattering letter, in expressing his regrets. He says, "My attention as an examiner was even then" (in college days) "strongly drawn to him, not only by his scholarship, but by the marked superiority of his intellect, and by the quiet self-possession, the mild dignity and grace, of his whole bearing." More "distant sentiments . . . soon passed, on *my* part, into those of warm personal . . . attachment." Finally, after many kindly wishes and foretellings, Mr MacDougall said, "May he prove in his new position the stay and encouragement, the genial counsellor and generous friend, of many a solitary student, who may be climbing painfully the arduous steeps of learning and of fame, and help . . . to shed around such, some portion of that affection and esteem which have so largely and happily accompanied his own steps." Whether or not these words from his former Professor ever reached the ear of Veitch, it seems clear that he looked upon his relationship to his own students as one of the most responsible bits of his life-work, and that he succeeded in no small degree in being, outside the class-room, both " genial counsellor and generous friend."

He used to groan over that percentage which inevitably in a large class showed neither caring nor capacity for his teaching—*i.e.*, for its subject. But many a time, when he came in to breakfast after the early class in Glasgow days, there would be an energetic glow in his face as he described " these good lads of mine," with their eyes turned to him where they sat in hundreds, silent and, as he hoped, receptive.

Professor Knight bemoans the decay, nay, the disappearance, of that hero-worship which,

he says, "every one once bestowed on their
philosophic teacher," and goes on : "If it be
true (as I think it is) that Veitch was never
regarded by his students as Hamilton used to
be, this was probably owing more to a change
in the *Zeitgeist*, in the academic spirit of the
time, than to anything else." This may be
so, although it is to be hoped that so serious
a change is more apparent than real. At the
same time, it is very unlikely that Veitch's
friends have ever thought of comparing his
influence among students with Sir William
Hamilton's. He himself would have smiled
at the notion.

For Sir William's in his day was a name
to conjure with : he attracted men to the
University of Edinburgh when many other
attractions held sway within it, and he had
that "singularly magnetic influence" to the
charm of which we all so delightedly yield.
Veitch was quite otherwise moulded, and it
was literally true of him that he passed his
real life "in the atmosphere of the unseen";
and "that a spirit so poetical, . . . so reveren-
tial, and even mystical, should have been linked
in one personality with an intellect so master-

fully acute, was the problem, as it was the fascination, of his character."[1] But he was no leader of men in the direct sense which goes with social qualities. It was foreign to him to attempt the modification of another mind in any conscious way. He let people be, and often lamented what probably he could have helped to change. Yet by a curious and rather touching contradiction he responded like a child to the demands made on him : he rejoiced in the smallest sign of affection shown to him in spite of his shyness and reserve. Himself the sincerest of men, he would even mistake the flatterer for the true lover; it was as if the hunger of his nature for sympathy in his kind led to a positive lack of penetration.

His students, ready as any others to criticise his teaching, and to find matter for laughter in his idiosyncrasy, give their own testimony as to the sway he held over them. Something very like love was expressed in the half-humorous name by which he went among them : "Daddy Veitch." No one watching them, while he addressed them, could doubt

[1] R. M. Wenley, Introduction to 'Dualism and Monism.'

I

that he carried them with him, lifted them with him, when a man less intimate with Scottish character, and less sympathetic with the young and aspiring, would have stranded them, and simply posed as an expounder of theories. His fine voice and delivery had their own value; but there was more than that, and it was found in the truth, purity, reality of the man before them. It was Dr John Brown who said of him, " He has the unconscious power of attracting young men to him, which makes him a master as well as a teacher, so that for his students *ito* is not required, *veni* is always enough."

Now, after his death, one of his last prize-men writes thus of him "whose memory I revere as I revere none others. I could never in words say how much I owe him. I had . . . never heard his voice till on the first day of the session . . . from the rostrum of the Logic class - room, in prayer. That prayer struck me and stuck to me. One felt that there was nothing perfunctory or rhetorical about it; it came from the heart. We felt the awe and earnestness of it. It was . . . for light on the problems that perplex

men's thoughts,—a prayer for forgiveness, for
' these sins of ours '—that was the phrase."
" Men speak of this prayer to-day who were
in his class years ago. Talking with a friend
the other day, he (the friend) said to me that
Professor Veitch was the greatest moral force
that had ever come into contact with his life,
and, with the exception of my own father, I
could say the same in truth. I have never
since his death heard a hard word said of
him. Students who differed from him in
point of view, reverenced him. One of them
lately said to me, ' There was nothing little
or weak about him ; he was a rock.' I thank
God . . . that I had the privilege of hearing
him. The dearest memories I have of college
life always take me back to the Logic class,
and I feel predisposed to a man who has an
affection for Professor Veitch." Yet another
student adds his description of that "pious
and lofty character." As to the daily prayer,
"one did not merely listen to what he said,
but was compelled by the earnestness of his
devotion to pray with him. . . . How real
was his faith in the actual presence of God,
how broad and generous his humanity, how

tender and large-hearted his sympathies! His influence came from the depth of great moral strength. . . . It was this stability that gave his influence power while he was present, and gives it permanence after he has passed away. I never felt his power and inspiration more real and living than I do now when he is dead."

Even reverting to the years when Veitch was still a student, and acted tutor to the boy John Macdonald (now Lord Kingsburgh), the same witness is given to his excellent influence. " I know," writes Lord Kingsburgh, " that his high example was providentially given to me in my early years, and that I cannot estimate how much I owe to it."

This, we notice, is all the man, and nowhere the philosopher. Better so; rightly so. Mr Wenley has already given us such an admirable study of Veitch's position in philosophy that any one reading, feels it as convincing as it is sympathetic. But to some of Veitch's friends it has seemed that the critical attitude which was normal to him as a teacher robbed him, so to speak, of a philosophical system of his own. Hamilton's, so widely imputed to him, was largely the accidental habitat of what in the student had to find expression, and what in the teacher could not be suppressed.

The fact that he had no solid constructive power in philosophy may have disappointed friends, but could be no discredit to himself. It could only, in the nature of things, come out after he took up the responsibility of Metaphysics as a Professor, and after he was bound to present to other minds the convictions of his own, as a pivot round which the rest of his teaching moved. As it turned out, he served well, but did not originate; and the remarkable way in which, unconsciously, he impressed himself upon others, only made it more clear that the philosopher went down before the engrossing individuality. Hamilton's was, of course, the only school of thought to which Veitch could be said to belong, but the fact has been too much emphasised for consistency with truth, and it was more because he could not be said to belong to any, that the fact of his having been trained under the Scottish Leibnitz led

people to consider that the mantle of that
Elijah had literally fallen upon this Elisha.

It must at least be taken into account,
that even under the imperial eye and over-
awing power of Hamilton, Veitch maintained
his own independence of mind, undisturbed,
erect, clear.   If then, young and a worshipper with the rest, "he retained his own
clear - cut, compact individuality,   .   .   .
being always more himself than Sir William's
or any one else's,"[1] we may fairly concede
that as he matured, he, of all men, was certain
to continue "always more himself."

A catalogue of works *may* be a man's least
title to fame, or, what is more important, to
the gratitude of his fellows.   But only one
who was blinded to the value of a laborious
mind of great logical acuteness, and the apparently thankless task of the weighty critic,
could demur to Veitch's rightful place in the
ranks of Philosophy.   We may in our minds
class such workers as he among the "hewers
of wood and drawers of water," but for that
very reason it is well to guard a judgment
which may so easily lapse into prejudice.

[1] Dr John Brown.

But it was evident to his friends, as Dr A. B. Bruce pointed out in kindly colloquy about him, that Veitch made a mistake, both as a teacher and a philosopher, in taking up an almost pugnacious attitude towards other philosophical systems and their exponents. At times, when he might have widened his sphere of influence, and perhaps done better by philosophy, he did not refrain from such intemperance of speech and attitude as was curiously anomalous. This could not but lay him open to criticism, and tended to force the student to a too narrow and definite choice in the very study, of all others, where the illiberal and merely scholastic should be driven out of court.

It is strange to think of; yet not all his acuteness, his training, his devotion, could quite redeem that falling away from the true spirit; and accordingly Philosophy made him not a son but a servant in her house. It is, however, a noble thing to be such a servant, and, as we have seen, he never swerved from the thoughts and the ambition which originally led him to give up everything rather than forsake that service.

Those who perceived these things were rather the more drawn to him. No man could have held his friends through good and evil report more faithfully and loyally than he. To realise this we have only to turn to the names of Nicolson, Shairp, John Brown, Fraser, Ramsay, Tulloch, Sellar, Knight, to read their letters and recall the look in their faces when they and he spoke together.

"To most men," says Professor Ramsay, " he was reserved and self - contained, or known mainly as the sturdy, uncompromising pro- pugnator of any question which he took up ; to me, and to some of his earlier friends, . . . he was as open as the day, con- cealing nothing, reserving nothing, mincing nothing, but pouring out his whole soul of ad- miration or contempt or ire upon books, opinions, or men, as he thought each deserving of them, in the most human and unrestrained of vocabularies." [1]

It was this torrent of utterance, this trust, this fine abandonment of himself, that endeared him to the chosen few ; and those who did not

[1] Scottish Mountaineering Club Journal, Jan. 1895.

at once strike response from him, were in not
a few cases rewarded for taking the trouble
to seek him out, by being suddenly accepted
in the inner circle, and given a place in his
affections which nothing but death could unfix.
Within that narrow circle the first friend of
his maturer years was undoubtedly Principal
Shairp; and it was in the St Andrews days
that they were so much together. "Amongst
all his colleagues," says Professor Knight,
"Shairp's influence at this time was probably
the most powerful, and the friendship between
these two men was intense and profound."
The harmony which could be felt between
them was of the most delicate nature: besides the love of brothers and the tie of mutual
interests, the very contrast of the two men
was one of balance, and each supplied in character the deficiencies of the other. Any one
who ever saw Shairp and Veitch walking up
and down the lawn at The Loaning, the taller
man with his arm thrown over Veitch's shoulder,
who heard their interchanging tones, or caught
the sight of each serene face, felt there was
something present upon which it was impossible
to intrude. They were the most spiritual of

lovers, and, in spite of grey locks, as gay and
as candid as boys. Walking through Oxford
together, where they once spent a charmed
week in each other's company, the contagious
spirit of the place seemed to fall upon them.
They would stand rapt before some sage's
portrait, or under some historic window; and
again, forgetting time and place, and passers-
by, would wheel round in discussion, as they
sallied forth from the quad of Oriel, and slap
each other's shoulders out of pure satisfaction
and good-fellowship.

It is easy to imagine that the influence of
Shairp gave special stimulus to that study
which Veitch took up afresh when he went
to St Andrews. English Literature was then
taught from his chair, and a more congenial
addition to his subject proper could not be
imagined. Knight, then in Forfarshire, used
to cross the Ferry and frequently spend a day
with Veitch; and to him, among Veitch's
other friends, it was apparent that at this
time there was deepening within him, not
only his knowledge of philosophy, but also a
great love of literature and romantic lore;

and alongside of these, the growth of that historic sense and antiquarian interest which he never afterwards lost.

A few side glimpses of his life at the beginning of his residence in St Andrews reach us in his letters to E. H. W.: of course they allude to work, but they also touch on events of the moment, and on his amusements and interests, along with more personal matters. One of the events was the famous Review (in Edinburgh) of August 7, 1860. Something of old James Veitch, the Peninsular warrior, seems to have stirred in his son, when he wrote as follows of "witnessing the Review, which was by far the greatest human spectacle I have ever seen. I never before experienced the same feeling in presence of my fellow-creatures as I did that day, or so vividly realised the fact of a common humanity. The whole thing was not only sublime, but so touching that I more than once felt inclined to shed tears. What a strong and mighty heart there is, after all, in this great nation, and how nobly that heart responds to the promptings of duty, and how fondly it clings to and cherishes

the love of our dear and blessed land! The
Queen, I am told, to her credit, gave way completely as the final cheer of her self-enrolled
defenders pealed like thunder from the valley.
. . . I was always sure I had a natural taste
for the soldier's life, but I have seldom, if ever,
felt the warlike stirring so strong within me as
on that day."

A year after, the tragic death of the Prince
Consort sent a wave of strong feeling through
the country; and within his narrow circle
Veitch had to mourn others. "Poor Cunningham," he writes, "is an irreparable loss
to the Church of Scotland, struck down too,
like the other [the Prince], in the prime of his
days, or little more. . . . I feel it as almost
a personal loss." Still nearer home came
the death of the father of his betrothed, "that
genial man," as Dr John Brown said, who had
such power of attaching people to himself,
whom his children adored, and with whose
generous spirit no man quarrelled. Indeed
this event postponed the marriage.

As to work, even before his induction he
writes of "that stupid Introductory Lecture,
which progresses provokingly slowly. . . . I

must be content to jog on in the dry round of
notions, judgments, and syllogisms, of which
it is best for people not to know even the
name. I am much afraid there will be a
large gathering on the 28th" (the day of
the University ceremonial). "This will make
the calamity greater than I looked for."
Again, "I am just beginning to see light on
the subject of my opening Lecture, but find
it hard and painful to elaborate the thing
fully, or so as to approach in the faintest
degree what I think it ought to be." "The
St Andrews people must think me an important person! . . . the bankers are making
application to be the depositories of my large
money account! I am also announced in the
Peebles paper among the '*Arrivals*'! On
seeing the announcement, my mother gave
expression to an ejaculation which betokened
very intense astonishment mingled with a
pretty large spice of contempt, . . . and then
drily remarked that the paper must be ill
off for news." This dry humour on the part
of the mother recalls another little incident of
slightly earlier date. A young lady meeting
her exclaimed, "So I hear John is engaged to

be married ? "   " Oh ! " was all Mrs Veitch
could say, for she had not heard the gossip.
" Pray don't say *I* told you," went on the
embarrassed friend.   " No, no," was the reply ;
" I'll just say I dreamt it ! "

It amuses us now, after hearing for years
his round abuse of sport and games, of tennis
and golf, and all kindred insensate follies, to
read from, " St Andrews, Jan. 26, 1861.   I
have begun *Golf*, so that J. —— may find
an antagonist of some powers on the Links.
My instructor in the art, ' Caddie — Geordie
Brown,' is *hopeful* of my progress, and en-
courages me to try my hand pretty often.
(*Aside*, he gets half-a-crown each time, which
of course doesn't affect his judgment in the
matter.)   Geordie backs me against Tulloch,
who, by the way, is about the poorest player
on the Links, and even anticipates that I
shall one day surpass him ! . . . Noble
encouragement !   However, Sellar and I go
out to-day to play . . . till dark."   Curling
and skating he liked in some measure ; but,
as every one knows, his membership of the
Peeblesshire Shooting Club had nothing to do
with the gun, but only with the social occasion,

and the pleasure of eating what other people had shot! In 1861 he can write thus : " I begin to feel a vehement desire for Tweedside and its freshening pastures. One day's fishing just now would be worth five pounds to me,— if indeed the value could be estimated in anything so vulgar as money." But even this once delectable occupation of every possible season was dropped, and became a lost art. It was superseded in his experience by the satisfying pleasure in Nature pure and simple.

There was much to engross the young Professor, but less even than usual to relate of him during the St Andrews years. His marriage occurred in June 1862, and we still have the hasty note pencilled by himself, and handed to his best man, Nicolson : " Married at 114 Princes Street, Edinburgh, on the 17th inst., by the Rev. Professor Douglas, Glasgow, John Veitch, M.A., Professor of Logic and Metaphysics, St Andrews, to Eliza Hill, only daughter of the late George Wilson, Esq., of Dalmarnock and Auchineden."

Two years later he was elected to the Chair of Logic and Rhetoric in Glasgow, which he held till his death. It was not, perhaps, the

happiest change of scene for him. Bred in
the high hill air of Peeblesshire, and fresh
from easterly sea breezes, the coming to
Glasgow had its drawbacks: but while he
never could like the city, he set himself to
find out and study its true life, east and west;
to search the Broomielaw and great shipping
yards; to tramp the suburbs and the curious
bye-ways of the town. He answered to all
within it with which he *could* sympathise.
Above all, the winter life there, and summer
life away, acted as foils to each other, and gave
zest to the work that belonged to each.

Then, too, as opportunity arose, he began to
indulge his love of travel. To companion him
through Germany to Switzerland, through
France to his favourite Northern Italy, who
could forget it! Ennui was unknown under
the stimulus of his fresh mind, and delightful
mixture of earnestness and fun. That companionship involved endless talk, and no
doubt he liked a good listener, a little weakness common to less good talkers than he.
Yet he could make it very nice for the listener.
" I have often sadly missed you," he wrote to
one who for ten years was his constant corre-

spondent, "and wished you with me. For one thing, that I might dash at the eccentricity of the momentary inspiration! How one does bang at things with sympathetic souls!" But there were times when he would fall into the silent mood, and, pacing in front of his companion, seemed lost to all about him as he brooded over the thoughts that arose within. Travel entertained and refreshed him in the limited yet enjoyable way he did it. But its most precious gift to him was the yearly enchantment of home-coming. For by this time (1868) he and his wife had built for themselves the house which was to remain their permanent summer home. It was simple and unpretending, and in these earlier years somewhat bare looking. But the trees which were planted by them have grown in the kindliest way, cared for year by year, and closely watched. Now the walls are clothed in greenery, and that nest-like feeling of home has gathered round and taken possession of every stone and tree. Mr Veitch chose the site, a bare field 700 feet above the sea, that he might have the upland feeling of his own country; he planned the windows, that he might live in

K

sight of Cademuir and Glensax: and it never seems to have occurred to him to build and settle in any but the place that had known him all his days, nor near any but those his "own familiar hills." As years went on he added to the original acreage a field here, a strip of land there, and ingeniously contrived, by humouring every bit of old hedge, and planting with a liberal but discreet hand, to give the spot a character of its own, a natural seclusion without the high walls he detested, and the primary charm it has, of merging with higher glades which carry the eye unbroken to beautiful Glensax, and the hill-tops that are fired with the summer afterglow.

Within the precincts no living creature might be trapped, however mischievous to garden or orchard. Fruits must be left to ripen without the selfishness of protecting nets. Flowers must live out their little lives, and the seedling broom which chance had sowed in the gravel of the drive was allowed to grow and spread as it liked. Birds, whatever their depredations, were welcome; all, from the stray cowslip which must not be weeded out of the lawn, to the hedgehog, the rabbit, the pheasant, the hare, and such friendly visitants, had "just as much right to live, and to live pleasantly," he would say, "as you and I." That the line was drawn at naughty boys with a predilection for green apples, and at hungry tramps who investigated (and changed) the appearance of the larder, was perhaps a pardonable inconsistency! With these exceptions, the despair of housewife and gardener fell on deaf ears. "Live and let live" was his motto, and, with all the consistency to be expected of a man who enjoyed good things, his practice!

His love of animals is too well known to need many words. But his position as President (in Glasgow) of the Society for the Prevention of Cruelty to Animals—and his dog-friend, without whom he never sallied forth in town or country—do no more than indicate the extraordinary tenderness he spent upon dumb creatures. I have seen him kneel beside a fallen nest of fledglings, and feed them from his own lip, talking pitifully the while. He would nurse a "lintie" that had flown against his study window, and next morning come down early to look after it, and set it free with trembling hand. One wintry afternoon in Glasgow he was coming home up the hill to No. 4 The College, through thick fog, when he heard before him the painful struggling and slipping of a cruelly laden horse. The carter lifted his foot and kicked the patient beast, and then swore and struck again, with "Curse yer soul!" Instantly a tremendous hand fell upon his shoulder, and a thundering voice of indignation stopped the words. "Man, do you know what you are cursing? It seems to me that your poor brute has more *soul* than yourself." Even in the half light the man changed colour; and the Professor put his strength to the back of the cart and saw the load to the top.

In the summer evenings, when his grey figure swung across The Loaning fields, after a long solitary ramble, the very cows would gather about him with the Swiss bells at their necks, and he would give a word to each by name, or stroke a favourite brown face, before he turned in by the well-known wicket-gate. "Petood" the college cat, and "Birnie" the college dog, who, as the gong sounded for dinner, rose and walked downstairs side by side before the company, were once familiar

THE PROFESSOR & HIS DOG "BIRNIE"

to many.[1]   Indeed his pleasure in animals
grew with his years, and dates from further
back than when, as a student at Biggiesknowe,
his cat, seated on his shoulder, watched him
write and read.

The return to Peebles, whether from St
Andrews or Glasgow, must have seemed very
natural and necessary after having done the
same during most of his student days.   But
we find that he added to his knowledge of his
home-country, especially during early Glasgow
years, by beginning in earnest what he called
his "Border raids."   Professor Ramsay says
that "one is half tempted to suspect that
it would have been more to his liking if nature
had made him a Border reiver instead of only
. . . a professor."   Indeed, when he started
off from his headquarters at The Loaning,
strangely garbed, and staff in hand, to wander
over the hills for days and nights alone, one
realised that wild old blood, and an irresistible
inbred love, mingled with the vagabondish
tendencies of the philosopher !   Here are a
few of his own flashing words after sundry
"raids" : "Driven by an impulse which means

---

[1] Comp. "Jockie," in 'Merlin, and Other Poems.'

reaction from the dry bones of the Valley of
Vision into which old Ezekiel kicked, I
buckled my knapsack, and with it and plaid
. . . went by Manor Head to Yarrow, staying
at Kirkstead with the Frasers. . . . I broke
loose on Saturday for many hours, . . . being
bound to the hard log of labour while sun and
clouds and breeze and—at length! the heather
bloom, were calling." Or again: "I go to
Kelso, to the Dinner of the Border Counties"
(Association), "there make a speech. . . .
Next day take knapsack for the hills of Teviot-
dale, disappear from human ken for seven days.
Oh! the joy! oh! the glory! The herds'
wives will give me scones, and I shall get
nooks to sleep in here and there. If, as may
happen, I yield up the ghost at the back of
a dyke, then 'Twa Corbies' 'on a stane' will
point to where the bones are to be found.
Isn't it nice that there are 'twa'? . . . But
I fear that Snake syllogism is going to eat
up all my summer!" Once more: "I had
a glorious walk to Loch Skene. . . . After some
hours, one a terrible fight with the peat-hags,
. . . I sighted the Loch. . . . You should
have seen . . . and wept for the lonely

joy. You know, if I were a woman and had
a lover, I should take him that walk by the
hags of Winterhope, and if he bogged (as is
exceedingly likely), I should leave him there
as a goodly riddance, and return home rejoicing in freedom from future tyranny and
cares !"

"Do you know," says a letter of later date,
after a certain "heart-stirring stretch," "that
an old automaton walked from the Douglas
Stones to The Loaning in three hours, burdened
with knapsack and plaid. . . . Alas! the years
that are on me, and the young heart that is
in me!" It was, as we know, long before
these heavy years, and while he was still
light of foot as of heart, that the "raids"
began and the habit of daily tramping across
country established. He was lost without the
afternoon with nature. "Summer and winter,
in town or in country, at home or abroad, it
mattered not ; through Glasgow fog, under
Highland mist or Italian sun, he must be up
and out to put himself in touch with pure free
nature, as he would call it, . . . something
that might put freshness and suggestion in
his heart, and drive the sense of work and

worry from his brain." [1] " No one who ever
enjoyed it," says Professor Knight, " could
forget a long country walk with Veitch. . . .
I remember once sitting with him far up on
the slopes of Manor Head at a green spring-
well, and reading to him some unpublished lines
of Wordsworth which had reached me shortly
before.   They touched him to the quick, and
led him on to talk, and to quote much from
other poets in a similar strain, as we wandered
on to Dollar Law, and descended on the other
side of the range.   He was at his very best.
. . . We traced out part of the old raiders'
road, and his conversation on the History and
Poetry of the Border was all touched by poetic
fire.   One felt how the warfare once waged in
these glens had made life eventful and full of
pathos ; how the people in them had been
reared in the sternest virtues of independence,
pride, and courage. . . . In the course of such
a walk one was more fully initiated into the
past history of the District than by poring
over many a printed volume."

Not only was this true, but it was done
with native freshness and ease, and the list-

[1] Professor Ramsay.

ener could not be oppressed by it. Like the
clear, quick waters of a hill stream, the
thoughts and associations which every turn
of the way awoke in his mind were poured
forth, now in murmuring tones, again with
impulsive gesture ; or, as he paused upon
the heights, reciting some martial ballad in
the ringing voice so stirring to hear, or wailing
out the laments and dirges of that "waefu'"
land. They were indeed his own ; and when
he chanted the verses or told the tales that
so absorbed him, no one wished him silent.
Who that heard it — and it was a great
favourite—forgets his saying of this ?—

> "As I gaed ower yon high, high hill,
>   And doun yon dowie glen,
> The roar that was in Clyde's waters
>   Wad ha' feared a hunder men.
> Oh roarin' Clyde, ye roar ower loud,
>   Yer streams seem wondrous strang;
> Mak me a wrack as I come back,
>   But spare me as I gang."

One would have thought that he himself was
the lover, with only one Fair Margaret in all
the world, and she a-dying on the other side
of the river. How he would repeat that last
line, "But spare me as I gang"! It was

not merely dramatic; it echoed in his own
nature, and he asked the question which to
him needed no answer, when he said, "Has
the intensity of the love-passion, or the daring of the human will, been more powerfully
expressed than in these simple words?"—('The
Tweed,' p. 220.)

No doubt Veitch candidly thought of himself as a poet and a philosopher, because he
passionately loved philosophy and the Muse;
but it must not be imagined that he thought
otherwise than humbly and simply of himself,
the man.   And although he became, in a
measure that few attain, what he had laboured
to become, his success had this true effect—
that it uplifted not himself but his standard
in all directions. "I?   What am I?" he
would say; ". . . of the earth, earthy." "I
am not good; I am a worthless old man."
"Ah me! wae's me! for what one ought to
have done—and been." Such phrases would
fall from the sincerest lips, and he would
extend the spirit of them to his writings,
questioning (not without reason) the worth
and correct form of his verses, and echoing
in his free, expressive letters the realisation

of his own smallness in the face of the things to which his heart and mind went out. There was something on the surface which struck his friends as combative, aggressive — as derived, very likely, less from character than the difficult nature of his upward early life; but to those who were much with him, he calmed and simplified himself, and dropped the crusty element which, as often as not, was mere disguise.

" While things go into yesterdays, they often live in to-day," was a sentence of his own, which was true in his experience. He did not merely in his letters, for example, describe nature and reflect in an abstract way which shut out other people. Rather he remembered the yesterdays, and was glad, if he could, alike to keep up the friendly usage, and to make good again a threatened bond. " I like to keep up a custom," he would say, "even of five years' standing. I am so bound by local and personal ties. Never was man more so— though I do not always own it ! "

What his students knew of his willing mind —and purse—to help them, many another also gratefully knew; and, looking back, he would

never, especially as an older man, grudge the
trouble of going over the familiar speculative
ground, or of strengthening by his own advice
and belief whatever he saw was honest resolve.
He was one of those men who are, in some
important respects, at their best in the company of women. He made friends of them in
more cases than one, exactly in the way in
which women of sense like to be friends. Of
course it will occur to some women, and many
men, that the source of this lay in his dominant
character combined with a nature not inac-
cessible to flattery! But this was not the
truth—whatever occasion the enemy may take
to blaspheme! Women liked him because of
that in him which instinctively they knew to
trust : to them—*i.e.*, to his friends among them
—he opened out with a candour the very surpris-
ingness of which had charm ; and he attached
them to him quite unconsciously by the pleasant
mingling of the comradeship which put them
on equal terms, and that chivalrous feeling
which in his clear soul placed the merest girl
that he liked on a pinnacle above him. "There
is something in having daughters," he says,
alluding to a visit of three lively girls who

teased and delighted him, "though they *are* frequently troublesome! Other people's are, I should think, best! This is enigmatical, I perceive, but not more so than a passage of Byron which John [Ruskin] in his Gospel, chapter viii., praises as grand English."

"A woman's life," he wrote, with the understanding we all appreciate, "is necessarily a distracted life; but the distraction may be, and is often, ennobled by that which distracts: *e.g.*, a readiness to seize opportunities of good, of help, sympathy, and cheerfulness, to those in need of them, is often very distracting, but it is ennobling. . . . Intensity in one line or piece of work is not necessarily a good, unless the work be good; and the work is never well, far less perfectly, done if it do not suit the faculty of the doer. A life may be frittered away on a single purpose—fruitlessly fulfilled in the end. In this case intensity may be no good, as distraction may be no evil. All that can be good is—Let a person, man or woman, try to find *what* is his or her special faculty, if he or she have one, which is not common, and follow it; bending circumstances as far as possible to its pursuit or development. If

circumstances demand time and strength, give
it, provided it can be given without self-re-
proach ; but see that there be no veneering of
mere inclination—which is often called duty.
. . . This you will find to be true : that
a single pursuit in life, be it literature, paint-
ing, art in any form, is a strength, a steadi-
ness, and a moral and intellectual culture for
the whole life, even if it be carried out under
the pressure of circumstances only fitfully."

Again, in reply to a prickly letter, born of
certain of his ironical taunts : " The emotions
are keen and quickened in the case of one who
worships an ideal, and they are apt to over-
flow and clothe things in their own colouring.
. . . At the same time I may say, it is
a conviction of mine that marriage relationship is overrated as a means of elevating
individual character, and while it *may* do so
— often does greatly — it does not *always*.
Further, there is a side of love, or lovers,
which naturally causes a smile. You will
find the theory of this in Adam Smith's
'Moral Sentiments,' where he deals with sup-
position . . . of the 'Impartial Spectator,'
whose emotions cannot be supposed to keep

hourly pace with those of the lovers, and
thus there arises a ripple of the ludicrous.
This is just the humour on the face of the
deeply genuine, and the deeper the more apt
to arise. . . . But perhaps I am not much
of an 'Impartial Spectator,' and enter into
your feelings more than you imagine, respecting both their depth, fruit, and genuineness."

A subject now comes up in which Veitch
took special interest—namely, the history of the
old name he bore. It cannot be established
that he was lineally derived from the old
Dawyck or any other noted Veitches. There
was at least one link which, as he himself admitted, fell out in the genealogy. Possibly it
is much like those flaws which a less veracious
antiquary than himself would have slurred
over, and which are in this way discounted
every day by persons who lay stress upon such
matters. But it touched his imagination not
the less, that for hundreds of years his name
had held some of the finest properties in the
Scottish lowlands, had been the support of
Scottish kings, and the terror of the lieges;
and he had some ground for his belief that he
belonged to them, however remotely, in fact as

well as in spirit. Probably the only unkindly
smiles over his open desire to know his forebears,
came from those who knew nothing about the
historical and antiquarian researches he had
made on the subject. Some friendly banter it
often evoked. Dr John Brown used playfully
to hail him " My dear Dawyck," and Professor
Fraser saw the " Modern Dawyck and Border
Wordsworth" in one, not from any faith in
the possible lineage, but rather from mingled
fun or teasing, with insight into that which
made him like Wordsworth in a true and good
sense, and like enough to be descended from a
famous and spirited people. Yet it was impossible not to sympathise with the wish of
the solitary, self-made man, to associate his
life by ever so distant threads with the indomitable race of La Vache—the men who
held the white shield with the sable heads
through centuries of feudal and national tur-
moil, and whose motto is to this day, " Famam
extendimus factis."

It was equally impossible, from the internal
evidence of his character and demeanour, to
doubt that he bore within him a nobility
not of yesterday. The integrity of mind;

the dignity unexpectedly shown; the gentle strength; the courtesy alike to the shepherd on the hill, and the stranger within his gate, —these showed it.

The subject of "Veitch," the name, history, and heraldry, was one of the interests which brought about acquaintance, and then friendship, with the late Sir John Murray Naesmyth of Posso. Sir John wrote frequently, and the exquisite site and glades of beautiful Dawyck were for long the terminus of the Professor's Saturday walk. Then Sir John, whose sympathy with trees, and artistic instinct in planting, strikes us still, even on a spot of great natural resources, would send young oaks to The Loaning, where they were treasured and sustained; and Mr Veitch would urge this antiquarian rescue, or that restoration of ancient pathway, not without success. Again, when Sir John put back to its rightful spot the font of St Gordian, adding a simple cross far up the lonely valley of Manor, the Poet of that Valley sang in simple verse, out of sheer delight in the relic restored!

As each summer brought round the day for

L

the open-air service at the Cross of St Gordian,
hardly a year, wet or dry, but he was there.
The occasion was one of primitive simplicity,
but indescribably touching and solemn : a wide
hush filled the solitary valley, and one at least
among those present might be seen rapt in
spiritual awe, and profoundly worshipping.
Nature and God were equally near, a double
Presence, glorious and overwhelming.

It was from Sir John Naesmyth that Mr
Veitch received the facsimile of the Veitch
arms, which he wore upon his seal ; and
through him also had access to the Posso
papers — these last leading him, we cannot
but suppose, to much more important results
than any mere point in genealogy. For it
drew his attention in a special case to the
history of the Border country, and immediately from that to its poetry. What had
always attracted him, now became his definite study, and the fruits are ours in the
best work of his life—viz., 'The History and
Poetry of the Scottish Border.' That, and
the 'Feeling for Nature in Scottish Poetry,'
were the outcome of his own interest and love
of the theme, which were so evident in his

letters, in his verse, in his daily life and habit,
but in no way with such valuable—and permanent—result.

It was not so much the "constitutional dislike of publicity" to which Mr Wenley refers,
that threw Professor Veitch in upon himself,
as it seemed. Rather it was his intense love
for the solitude which gave him time, and the
luxury of yet more time, for reflection; love,
too, for the uplands of his own country, which
to his historic sense and poetic vision were
peopled indeed, and worth to him all the fine
cities in the world. In thanking Principal
Shairp for his just and friendly notice of
the Border Book (first edition), he adds, "It
needs all the help that can be given to it
extraneously; sensation is . . . too strong
for reflection in this modern world of ours.
. . . The still small voice is very apt to be
discouraged,"—a remark which shows that he
was not unable to measure the real scope of
his best work; although there were times when
he showed a lack of the same discrimination
about his less valuable efforts.

It is true, as Mr Ramsay has said, that to
realise the "solid work" which Professor Veitch

has done " in the way of analysing and illustrating the sentiment for Nature-beauty, of showing what part external nature has played in moulding the thoughts, lives, and legends of our Border ancestors, we must study 'The Feeling for Nature in Scottish Poetry' and 'The History and Poetry of the Scottish Border.' The former book deals with the theory of the beautiful, and traces through the whole range of Scottish poetry the varying and progressive modes in which, at successive periods, the objects of our natural scenery have appealed to the hearts . . . of men. The latter book "—which, it may be added, seems to his friends the better of the two—" is a monumental collection of the most characteristic incidents and freshest poems of Border life reduced to a unity of feeling by a highly sympathetic imagination." " Many an evening," says its writer, " of poring over old documents this volume has cost me ; and many a day under lowering as well as sunny skies have I spent in seeing for myself the scenes of the historical and traditional incidents." [1] Evenings and days, these, spent truly *con amore!*

[1] History and Poetry of the Scottish Border, Preface, first edition.

Books of course must speak for themselves; but only such as find readers can be said to be given their chance. The book reviewed, the book abbreviated, the book talked about, and skimmed over—not one of these common weeds is in the least to be accepted as the book *read*. The injustice, often unintended, of discussing what we do not know, is the heaviest we can inflict on a writer, whether come to fame or not likely ever to do so. People otherwise conscientious are often stupid, and even heartless, about this. Pretended interest is worthless, but if we care enough for a man and his book to consider it with him, should we not do the dead, at all events, that obvious courtesy of reading before we pronounce?

Local, the interest of the Border Book undoubtedly is; but its appeal, if it extend no further, is to all Scottish men and women; and for them it would be gain but to follow the example, and avoid the reproach, of these its author's words: "Since I came back from The Loaning there has been the usual daily darg" (burden), ". . . not unpleasant, . . . and I have been able too, in a desultory fashion, to keep up old Scottish poetic feeling and history

in my mind, with now and again fresh glimpses
into that quaint life, language, manners, and
feeling, of which especially Scottish men and
Scottish women are most ignorant."

It was in 1878 that the familiar green
volume, best of guides and companions to
the Border counties, came out. "Here she
is!" cries Dr John Brown on receiving a
copy, "comely, sonsy, in her olive green. It
is a beautiful book, and I like its plump-
ness. . . . I hope it will be popular; it
should. But it is in some ways too good for
the many; and yet one hopes it . . . will
revive the poetry of human nature, of the
people, of flesh and blood, of nature, and let
us get away from quasi-philosophies and in-
trospections, and unwholesome sensibilities.
Scott and the ballads for ever! . . . All
victory to the book and its cause!"

Considering Mr Veitch's close retention all
his youth by the most exacting of studies, it
is not surprising that he did not begin to *sing*
until the age at which the majority of rhyme-
sters cease. The wonder rather is that, beginning after the full swing of life was upon
him, he should have sung at all. Surely it

was the sign of a heart at leisure from itself.
Not a trace remains, at any rate, of any poem
earlier than those which appeared in 1872 as
'Hillside Rhymes.' These, followed by 'The
Tweed, and other Poems,' in 1875, and by 'Merlin, and other Poems,' as late as 1889, make up
his offering in verse to the lovers of Tweedside.

Between his friends these volumes were in
turn the subject of what Dr John Brown called
"cordialisations." They were greeted with
hearty and encouraging criticism by men like
him and Shairp, by Fraser and Masson and
Sellar. They were read and praised, and in
some minds gave birth to a hope that their
writer would rise above the level which divides
talent from inspiration. When unfavourable
reviews appeared—and they did appear—John
Brown simply said, "It was, and is, a pity;
but you are a philosopher, and can afford to
despise. I wish I was a philosopher!" And
then by another post he would write in cheerful strain, "Have you seen Skene's excellent
letter on Veitch's book?" ending with charming irrelevancy, "My dear Poet, . . . happy
are you to fall asleep under the shadow of the
Hundleshopes!"

Principal Shairp, who had seen parts of the
'Hillside Rhymes' in proof, liked best the
"Manor Water" and "Manor Head in Winter."
But two others in the book came up to these,
in his opinion. "'Hay of Talla' is one of the
most concentrated pieces of weird, unearthly
grimness I know; and the last, 'Alta Mon-
tium,' blends, finely, keen insight into the
nature of the hills with . . . abstract
thoughts. It is peculiarly *you*. There are
differences in point of execution and felicity,
but . . . all are the *real* thing."

Principal Shairp's letters are written with
such affection, interest, and patient trouble,
that they must have given Veitch real help.
For they are discriminating and often severe;
and he gave chapter and verse for his plain
speaking.

In one letter, when 'The Tweed' appeared,
he sends a "sample of minute verbal criticism on ten first pages," and a long careful
letter of suggestions: "It is so full of true
solid poetic ore, that I wish to see it set
forth in the best outward form. . . . You
see how free I am in making criticisms. It is
because I believe in the poem and in you that

I make bold to do so." "No doubt," says
another of his friend's letters, "you are by
nature, and should be, a poet : you have but
to study the 'accomplishment' of verse, which
of course needs practice." When the subject of
publication came up, Shairp wrote, "I cannot
say how far they will take with a public sated
with sensational writings. But to 'natural
hearts' they will afford, as they have done to
me, true and refreshing pleasure, and I believe they will do no discredit to your name."
He criticises points "for which I don't know
the rule, but which one's ear judges of," forgetting his friend's lack of ear ; but goes on,
"And whatever the world of London, or even
Edinburgh, may say, I think they will be
cherished in Tweedside, high and low, long
after you and I have ceased to hear its mur-
mur—unless Scotchmen are wholly changed."

There were admittedly one or two friends
who shook the head, or were silent, about this
poetry-writing : one at least treated the verses
with scepticism because they transgressed the
laws of music, and were given over to monotonous abstraction in limited vocabulary. But
the spirit in which Mr Veitch received criticism

from such as Principal Shairp bore out his own words, "The kindest of all things is to tell a man (or woman) his or her faults—*i.e.*, those that seem to you to be such. Is this not giving them of your own life-earnings?" It is clear, from the letters, that other men criticised more generally, yet on the same lines as Shairp, and felt about them on the whole as he did. But by a simple enough paradox it remains a fact, that the friends who could best know and value his work were the very persons who, knowing himself, cared least to read him. As Shairp said, so said they all; the real merit or demerit did not greatly affect them. If they liked his verse, one of its attractions was, "It is so truly *you!*" If they were indifferent to it as poetry, still they said and felt, "It is so truly *you.*" Like the verdict of his students upon his philosophical teaching, which affected them infinitely less than his personality, so is that of his readers, as far as poetry in verse is concerned.

But this brings us to the most important fact in Professor Veitch's life, the value and happiness of which it is good to know he realised. It is not easy to put the fact into

true words. Many men have walked with
Nature, entered into fellowship through her
with the Unseen, rejoiced in simple things,
and been stronger and purer for it. But the
relation which existed between John Veitch
and Nature was one of unusual closeness and
intensity. One might say without exaggera-
tion that this bond was the deepest in his
experience, he himself being unaware of its
depth, although he well knew its delight.
Nature never palled upon him, never oppressed or fatigued him. More than from any
human resources (and these he did not lack),
he found the only liberty he valued, liberty of
thought, serenity of mind, fellowship of spirit,
in his communion with hills and " hopes." He
was out of his element in city life ; yet even
there, perhaps the more, he caught at every
touch of Nature's hand in street and suburb.
In one letter, referring to the annual move in
October, he says, " Amid rain and irritation . . .
straight to foggy Glasgow ; yet all the way "
(in spite of " rain and irritation," generally
spoiling to scenery) " the autumn was glorious
and pathetic . . . up to the coal-pits of Lanark-
shire, when only the naked arms of trees—

waeful trees— . . . were horrid against the
sky. . . . Manufacturing industry has much
to answer for.   It has cursed this country,
and deprived thousands of their natural sus-
tenance—the light of heaven and the greenery
of earth."

Work was essential and natural to him; but
in Glasgow, in spite of work, he at times fell
out of spirits.   "I am pithless now, from darg
and hack—only roused to activity by extreme
opposition, and then there is a flame—but it is
abnormal!   I must set to my day's darg, and
see what I can squeeze out of an old brain!"

"I believe there is weather here, but I
really do not know or care what it is. . . . I
have a profound impression that the whole
nation is going to the bad—what with tricky
Toryism, and Opportunism, and flabby Glad-
stonianism, windy and weak.   Bah! oh for a
man!"

Again, "The dinner at 'Blank's' . . . was
inelegant but full.   'Blank' is really very good,
very kindly, but the ideas!—I go to the
Architects to-night to discourse on Glasgow
architecture—*i.e.*, boxes with holes, for bailies
and millionaires and their wives!   Write to

me soon—I am very cross with myself; let me commune with you." These are a very few of the phrases in winter letters, which echoed his mood. But there was another and a bright side even to Glasgow weather, especially in his early years there. For in 1864, as far back as the year of his election to the Logic Chair, the mutual love of the hills brought Professor Ramsay and him together. "The close intimacy which sprang up between us," writes the former, "remained unbroken until his death, and his friendship for me had all that peculiar charm which attaches to confidence and affection extended by an older to a younger man."

Such passing glimpses of nature as he could get in afternoon and Saturday walks, pacified and sustained him. As early as 1866, or about then, he and Professor Ramsay and Mr Campbell Colquhoun of Clathwich formed what they called the "Cobbler Club." They were its sole members, and its object was to promote the climbing of every hill-top that could be reached from Glasgow in winter-time, within the limits of a Saturday excursion. "The name had nothing to do

with shoe-leather,—it came from the gallant
Argyleshire hill of that title, which in those
days was . . . supposed to be the most distant top" within their limit. "In this way
many a good height was scoured over, from
Tinto to Ben Lomond, from Dunmyot to
Dungoyne, from Earl's Seat to Neilson Pad,
in weather of every kind. Many were the
cracks we had with country folk by the way,
many the snug old farmhouses penetrated for
shelter or information. In the evening, full
of holiday and hill air, we would gather some
choice souls together, and hold in high fashion
the Professors' Saturday Night, unhaunted by
the spectre of an early class with its angry
bell upon the morrow." And year after year
this was true of him, as his friend has
also noted, "I have seen him take more delight in watching a sunset from Buchanan
Street than most of those who jostled him
were capable of taking in from the most
beautiful scenery in the world."

"I have had now and again quiet walks,"
he would write, "westwards towards the sunset over the Argyle hills. . . . They are far
off, but still they have often glowed as

they did that afternoon we saw them." As time went on the "quiet walks" were curtailed, the Glasgow life became narrower, and he fretted under the limitation of lessening strength, besides showing the greater eagerness to be gone to Peebles.

While still a man in his fifties, he had the sorrow of seeing friend after friend go from him, and he, more than most men, neither could nor wished to make new ones. "Very sad to me," he writes, "is this passing away of Tulloch. Ferrier, Shairp, Tulloch, Sellar, and myself, these were the five consorting in St Andrews twenty-six years ago! . . . Sellar and I alone remain — for how long or short one cannot tell." To lose such friends as Sheriff Nicolson and Principal Shairp alone would have meant peculiar grief to any man; to him who attached himself so fervently to the few it was piercing.

On the beautiful September morning when he suddenly saw Shairp's death in the papers, he was stricken through the heart, and could not at first utter even the groan that came to his relief. "I have not," he wrote soon after, "for many a day been so benumbed by a blow. The heart seems to have gone out of me for work, thought, almost feeling. Alas! for my brother beloved; for a man more soul to soul, heart to heart—with me —I have not met in this world, and do not expect to see again. Into the 'sunless land' —well, it is sunless enough to my eyes. I see not, know not, what and where it is. Yet there is a hope, even a faith, that no true pure soul is lost or engulfed in indefinitude—but lives; otherwise this universe is profoundly, essentially, cursedly irrational. Why should we be but to be the best? and if the best perishes, then what a mockery!" And when death cut off not only the elder friends, but dealt him heavy blows among the young also, the change came upon him which we see in most lives, the settled look created by grief, the look of one living apart and belonging to something to which we have no key.

The death of his gifted fellow-Borderer and loved child-friend, the "Laura" of whom he so touchingly writes, was to him, as to many who knew her less, a bitter loss;[1] and when,

---

[1] "In Memoriam : Laura," p. 134, 'Merlin, and Other Poems.'

a year later, another girl-friend and corre-
spondent was suddenly snatched from him, it
seemed to shake him to the core. He clung
the closer to what he still possessed.

But he did more. Sadder and quieter, he
mellowed insensibly, like the fields he loved,
preparing for harvest. New gentleness came
over him; he grew more tolerant, less hasty,
more genial to those with whom he really felt
out of touch, and more endeared to his own.

"For the past forty years no form had
been so familiar as his in the long summer
days on every hillside, by every stream, of
the Border country."[1] True; but the feeling for nature became now a craving and a
passion, where it had been only the deepest
pleasure and stimulus. The upland solitudes,
their wild recesses and unrecorded loveliness,
were now, so to speak, a foretaste of heaven.
But for the Dead, and the sorry inconsistencies even in Nature, he desired no better.
Many a time he said this; and, looking at
his face with the awe and light upon it, as
he paused on some hill-top, it was seen to
be truly transfigured.

[1] Professor Ramsay.

M

His letters of the last twelve or fourteen years are everywhere touched with the growing nature-intimacy which placed men and women and books and other interests on secondary, though not inferior, levels. No one could be jealous of that supremacy.

He had no knowledge of botany, although in a general way interested by the science which attracted his friend and neighbour, the late Professor Dickson of Hartree. Of geology he picked up stray axioms from Professor Geikie. The stars were, as far as he was concerned, unnamed. But while every fact bearing on the ways of nature interested him, his own interest was unaffected by such knowledge, and did not require its evidence of the marvellous. It was rather that he found a mind, and held communion with that mind, in every phase and aspect of nature,—from the rock-rose, "dear child of the sun," to the sun itself—"the fine touch of the hot summer day, the *sun's hand upon one's own*, link of a far-off companionship." The Well-Bush in Manor Valley is, he says, the "centre of my world." He would always pause in passing through that charming spot, with its

climbing natural wood, and bank of yellow
iris, and the trickling spring, ice-cold on the
hottest day. "What think you?" says another
letter; "in Manor from the Well-Bush wood
. . . a cuckoo greeted me exactly on the
day and spot he greeted me last year! . . .
That was worth a London gallery! and infinitely more worth than any 'Silver King'
gaslights and gamboge!" Another day it
is, "All the heavens are alive with motion
and interspersed with blue, . . . a de-
licious nor'-wester — chiefly wester." "Oh!
how delightful it was to be wild once
again, swinging one's arms and . . . stick,
without the risk from the odious crowd of
being put down as a lunatic! *Odi profanum
vulgus,—et arceo!*" Again: "The Linn was
quiet, . . . ending in a deep dark pool,
as many a life does, and as the Border
widow's did. But why not? Did it not
transfer its grief to the heart of humanity,
and why shouldn't it now be quiet? . . .
In the afternoon I went up the Watch Hill,
slick to the top—what think you of the old
dog, or devil?—and had the most superb
revelation of the southern slopes of the giants

from Dollar Law to Broadlaw! And then
. . . the moorland grass! Never finer. . . .
'Oh! the *splendour* of the grass'!" It was
of Manor Valley that he exclaimed:—

> " Life's deeds and words here fade and pale,
>   Thou dreamland of my living years. . . .
>   The memories of the higher self,
>   All that the grave can never claim,
>   All that the immortal cares to keep—
>   This thou alone for me canst name."

But still nearer home, at his very doorstep,
the same kind of feeling prevails—

> " Each chequered pane hath its own heaven; "

and from the "book-room" so familiar to his
friends, where he always worked, he looked
out on a favourite sycamore—

> " The figure always 'gainst the void,
>   To me more than a human friend."

Not less so was the pine—

> " That under open sky unsheltered draws
>   Its spirit from the blast."

Part of the charm of the summer life lay
in the coming home from his rambles, often
at eccentric hours, and with utter disregard
of gongs and dinner. He would catch the
"moon - eyed clock" far down in the High

"THE BOOKROOM"

STUDY AT THE LOANING

Street of Peebles, as, darkness about him, he rounded the top of Cademuir, and often chuckled to himself at the frenzied state of mind to which such a master must reduce his cook !

> " But lo ! another sight, a window lamp,
>   Descried across the fields, amid the trees,
>   Kept brightly shining by love's hand, to light
>   The homeward way ; and there a sweet, fair face
>   Solicitous, and keeping watch."

The summer, chiefly spent at The Loaning, was broken up in many pleasant ways. Besides the spring travels abroad, which were made to include London, and frequently brought him home by Devonshire, or Wales, or the Lake Country, there were visits to the North : to Phesdo, to the late Dr Burns, for whom he had a deep regard ; to Loyal, where he and Professor Ramsay could walk their wildest ; to the shooting quarters of various relatives and friends. And nearer home, in short flights to Gorton, and Hartree, and Thirlestane ; to Lamington, Dawyck, and Glen. It is like him that, visiting Dr Burns, he writes not of Phesdo, nor of the Grampians, but of his own hills — not,

however, forgetting genial words about his
kind host. "They [the Grampians] look
sombre and imposing, but lack the buffs and
browns and greens of our Tweed and Yarrow
hills. One is the better for seeing them.
They enhance the feeling of delicacy inspired
by the Border hills." On one occasion the
house party at Loyal had all gone to a
ball; but, he adds, "I had a very pleasant
evening here with a Tweedside lass, . . .
as cultured and Borderly susceptible a woman
as I have met with for long. Ah! the soul!
the soul! That is life.—Aye yours in the
old affection. J. V."

Balls and routs were of course utterly foreign
to his ideas of enjoyment : merely to be in a
crowd was penance to him. Yet his love of
the young, and his liking for the spectacular,
combined to carry him from time to time out
of his own quiet places. Then the old merri-
ment would show itself, and he wore an expression half deprecating, half amazed, which
betrayed his thoughts as clearly as if he
spoke! Yet he liked to be missed, even
while he wondered how his friends could
miss from social gatherings an old fellow

like himself! "Of course you have been riding the London wave : well, enjoy it when you can,—and if you can." "If you can" was his natural reflection.

Again : "Home I came from Yarrow—yes, Yarrow—last night, . . . after the play and the gaieties and the ghost-stories . . . on the night of New Year's Day." He had escaped! "I was resolved," the letter naïvely goes on, "to spend the next day in a *blessed* way." So he made for Yarrow across country, and thence home, mid-winter though it was. "The grey old warrior stream had risen in strength, and was pouring three ordinary Yarrows all the miles of way. . . . And yet there was an undertone of wailing, without which strength is rude and brutal. . . . It charmed, cheered, and softened me." "There had been a fall of snow through the night, the hills were under bright sunshine, and every head and crest and fold are as fine as if they had been spread for angels' feet." "Do you know, I think the appreciation of snow scenes shows the highest advance in refinement of æsthetical feeling. It does not delight in mere colour. It approaches the refining, delicate, purifying sense of form which is in sculpture."

All this living with nature constituted his true life. Such extraneous circumstances as his membership of various societies which interested him, or were interested by him, had small bearing on that life. Yet we know from the records of these institutions and societies that he worked for them steadily, and that his eloquent power in speaking was as much in evidence among them, as it had been in old days when he excelled as a student, whether to awake sympathy or to criticise reform.

But it was when water schemes threatened his "Dreamland," Manor Valley, that the full power of fighting and denouncing came out. Great and just was his wrath! From all sides, except of course that water-craving section of Edinburgh represented in Mr Veitch's eye by an unknown monster of iniquity, one "Bailie Baps," he received very practical sympathy. There is little doubt that he saved Manor from a great reservoir wall across its beautiful lines, and that he proved at personal trouble and expense the "peaty" nature of the water, as well as the fact that were it good for use it was to Peebles burgh it should run.

Dr John Brown was of course an abettor. "Curse ye bitterly," he wrote, " the schemes against Manor ; cursed be they in their basket and store, in their incoming and in their out- going ! But blessed be the Birkies of Dundee who vote for S——, and send that impudent Quack and his Baby back to their den ! " The scheme for Edinburgh is, as all know, now going on ; but it is at Talla lakes, far up Tweed, where the natural lake-bottom is still a morass, and where re-filling with water will enhance the beauty, without even touch- ing the character of the spot. Professor Veitch lived to know that " the sweetest stream of all the south " was untouched by the spoiler. He mourned over Talla too, but recognised in the temporary depredations a final benefit without destruction of local beauty.

He constituted himself natural guardian to all the old peel towers and romantic buildings or historical remains of his county, and even beyond it. Neither " Justice of the Peace "

nor "Doctor of the Laws" gave him anything like the satisfaction of his uninitiated
office! When a wayward rowan appeared
high on Dryhope Tower, and threatened the
stonework, a letter pleading the cause of old
story went off that evening to the owner,
and soon the harmful seedling was cut down.
With jealous eye he guarded every stand-
ing-stone from plough or tourist; and with
generous assistance of his neighbour, Miss
Kidd of Glenternie, he repaired and recovered
the dungeons and remnant wall of Castle Hill,
which, beautiful for situation, commands the
whole valley of Manor, and which belonged
in olden times to the family whose name
was also his.

One of his last services to us in this way
—and the interest of it is more than merely
antiquarian—was his prompting and promot-
ing a scheme by which the tower of Thomas
the Rhymer, called Ercildoune, was bought,
and became the property of the Border Counties Association. This was done as late as
1894, and again we are glad to think he
lived to learn that his suggestion would be
carried into effect.

His efforts to retain the landmarks of the past were not without result even in Glasgow. He took great interest in the removal, stone by stone, of the Gatehouse of the Old College, and its restoration at one entrance of the New; and many a time, as he passed up the "Lion Staircase," also removed from its old site, into the College quadrangle, he would pause to express his lasting satisfaction over a relic preserved.

It was one day in March 1892 that some among those who loved Professor Veitch most deeply, suddenly realised that an overshadowing something was upon him. He had been ailing, unlike himself, somewhat wan and weary-looking; but not till that day when he returned from the new-made grave of his college-friend and brother-in-law, Mr George Wilson of Dalmarnock, did the presage of coming fatality seize upon the heart. "Thou to-day, I to-morrow," he then said, as if to himself, with a look not to be forgotten. But neither he nor any one had any reason in fact to make them anxious at that time. He worked as usual; he went here and

there, felt better, then not so well; re-
visited St Andrews, where he addressed the
Philosophical Society of the University, and
planned with Mr Knight an expedition to
Flodden which never took place, for he himself had passed away before the time came
round. People were not aware of change in
him. "The vivid manner in which, in our
last long conversation, he described the battle-
field, . . . was as powerful a bit of descriptive speech as anything I ever heard. It
recalled Thomas Carlyle at his best." Again,
in Mr Knight's words, "I can never forget
how he then dealt with the questions which
few philosophers will ever face, in colloquial
discussion with their fellows — viz., those of
Theism and Immortality."

His letters, however, took a different tone,
unconsciously. "Out of sorts, out of heart,
and even soul, one has been for weeks, and
even now the tide is not quite turned. The
Lakes were very good in their way, and one
day from Grasmere *I strove against fate*, and
walked up 'far Easdale,' . . . rounded
the Langdales, saw many wee weird tarns,
. . . and so swung back. Since then I

have buried myself in work, and done Manor
almost daily, having there drunk in the green
soul of the hills. . . . What of destiny
or predestination in things? Nothing—unless
one accepts it, and only as one accepts it.
Old, dear, and beautiful James I. (of Scotland), back in the far centuries, put it all
in one stanza :—

> 'Fortune is most and strongest evermore
> Where least foreknowing or intelligence
> Is in the man.'

Read *woman*, it is the same, and for intelligence read *personality*, and you have the
key to the course of many a life. . . .
Œdipus! Œdipus! the puzzle!" Then, reverting to the never-failing interest, he speaks
of having "finished off old Drummond of Haw-
thornden, one of the finest souls of the whole
batch of Scotsmen," and of having been
"steeped for weeks in old romance! Why
on earth cannot we make a world such as
these old rhymers feigned? It was a true
and heavenly protest against—prose."

Gradually, but with sure hand, illness
settled upon him; and in May 1894 he received sentence, and returned for the last

time to The Loaning, knowing himself a
doomed man.

Up to this time he had been subject to
hours of deepest depression; there was a
haunting expression in the eyes; and he
would chafe impotently and cry aloud, "Why
should I, of all men, be cursed with this
awful disease?" But from the hour when,
with outward calm and great dignity, he
took the dire message to heart, his demeanour in these respects changed. "God's will
be done," he wrote to a friend. He spoke of
it openly; then set himself in silence to face
it, and bore himself with extraordinary courage. Wasting pain and misery swept over
him, but the strong spirit and will rose up
and sustained him. He went about his papers,
deliberately arranging everything he could.
He burnt letters, and pulled out old relics,
only ceasing when that which had to be
done was done. At the letters of his dead
friends he was induced to pause: it was too
much for him. "Ah me!" he cried, "these
are all from dead men's hands."

This done, he continued his day's routine,
as strength allowed, exactly as usual. When

moments of bodily anguish overtook him, he seemed to prefer to be alone; yet even then he would rouse himself, if any one wanted a word with him. Once or twice he would turn round, and without a word gaze into a friend's face, with a strange look, as if noting something for remembrance.

Again, or for a rare instant, he would give way, and with a low voice exclaim, "Only God knows the awfulness of this!" But as a rule he came and went, drove and strolled about, dined and read and talked of an evening as was his wont. Only for a moment now and again did he speak of what was coming—of the time "after I am gone,"—and then in a perfectly simple, quiet way. The mystery was much nearer him than even we knew.

When he felt unable for his usual reading he took to lighter books, and would sometimes even let these fall on his knee, to gaze out of the windows, of which, more than ever that lovely, sad summer, "each chequered pane had its own heaven."

One day the old longing, always present, overcame his sense of suffering, and he decided once more to visit Yarrow. There by a strange and happy coincidence he met his friend Professor Campbell Fraser. It was at the Gordon Arms (where Hogg bade his last farewell to Scott) that their last parting took place. "Even the partings are getting fewer," Mr Veitch had said a little while before. It was a cheerful group of friends, but with very troubled hearts among them. But as the visit went on, he, who looked so ill at first, revived, and threw himself into the spirit of the hour. It was a wonderful achievement. He kept the table in laughter, pretending to eat, and glancing up in the old keen way, as he caught at threads of conversation, and gave the repartee to his old friend. He walked out and let his ear catch once more the rippling of Yarrow, and with hearty words and smiles he bade good-bye. No one could have guessed what was hidden in his mind. Twelve days after that he lay dead in that upper room, his face towards the hills.

"Death then ended," writes Professor Fraser, "a companionship which, for nearly half a century, added largely to the happiness of my life, leaving the grateful remembrance of a unique personality—so true and good, so pure and beautiful, in the highest type of Scottish character, never to be forgotten."

Last farewells, last words, are too sad for rehearsal, however precious to memory. Let us reflect, however, that only in some instances was our friend aware that these were the last. He knew he would never see Yarrow again; he did not know that it was for the last time, when, four days before his death, he drove up Manor. The yearning expression in his eyes was tragic to see. "Would to God," he would exclaim, "I could once more stand upon these heights!" Nearly every evening of that August we used to gather about his chair, and he would eagerly follow, step by step, the ground one among us had walked that day. He would question every mile of it : he seemed to know every yard. No paths or landmarks were needed for him. He identified in memory every nameless spring, the pools of the upper burns, the ridges of the far-off "grains," and tried to repeat in another's experience the bygone delights of his own.

Then, before the evening was far gone, he would rise and bid us good night: " You must excuse an old man; for one *is* an old

N

man now - a - days." He was not yet sixty-
five.

This went on till one day, Friday, the 31st of
August (1894), on the evening of which there
was no gathering, save of anxious faces. On
that day Professor Ramsay, whose brief visit
had given great pleasure and cheering to his
friend, said good-bye. Next day was one which
it is best to commit to silence. Sunday broke
in all the still splendour of early autumn; the
hills were in their most sumptuous purple.
It was as if Nature were holding some high
and sacred festival. There was none of the
feeling of mockery with which she meets poor
mortals in trouble. Within, — the struggle
done as far as conscious and indomitable mind
could do it,—great quiet reigned.

"Ah! you have come," he said to me—for
it was an old promise—"and you will not go
away?" Long before, during one of the hill-
walks, he had said too: "When my time comes,
I should like just to lie down at the back of
a dyke, *on the heather.*" And so, on the day
which all his friends recall — when his body
was laid to earth—the grave did not look like
a grave at all, but only a dip in a hilly place,

where the harebell of his mother's fields nodded
here and there in the close, fresh heather.
That was brought from the slopes of Cademuir
by the faithful hand of his old and valued
servant, his gardener for five-and-twenty years,
who took a share in the last sad offices, and
followed among the friends that mourned, with
a heart as full as theirs.

Not the most indifferent spectator could
forget that last crossing of the Tweed: the
throbbing sound of many slow feet; the
champing of horses' harness; the spaced-out
tolling of a bell that seemed to echo in the
hills; and, above all, the musical rush of
broad waters. The old burgh left its work,
and stood by reverentially. All passed close
by the home cottage of Biggiesknowe, up the
narrow Old Town, into the green high-lying
spot, to the wall where the trees overshadow.

Gently the coffin, lowered by hands that
had clasped his, brushed the heathery sides—
and rested. *He had his wish.*

Tears, and flowers, and kindly Mother Earth
—who does not know it all, too well?

Already the white stone that marks his

place is toned and stained by sun and rain. The men and women who followed him to the grave are drawn back into the absorbing stream of daily life. To some even of those, he is become a mere name. For others he creates a daily blank. To one the light is gone out.

A man must stand or fall in the memory of his fellows on his own strength, and the inward virtue and service of his life. Least of all can those who loved him dictate the terms to others in which he shall continue theirs for help and inspiration.

But long ago, while still a student, working his way, as he ever did, to the best within his reach, he wrote a letter, which seems to give us in a few sentences not only his estimate of the noble in life, but our estimate also of the noble in him. It is dated from Peebles, May 2, 1858 : "I find a Sabbath here a very good thing for restoring me to the even tenor of my thoughts, and a sort of realisation of my own individuality, which are apt to be broken up and lost in the hurry of minute and harassing labour.

"Work is an ennobling thing, be it ever so humble—and I should never wish in this world to be independent of it ; but there is no lesson which it teaches more efficiently than just this : That, taken by itself, no occupation a human being can put hand to is a sufficient employment and gratification of all the capacities of his nature. That part of divinity which is in us will not be satisfied with finite products, and *must* have something more than all we can ever reach on earth. . . . There is nothing I sympathise so readily with as the simple quiet of a green field or budding wood, which seems to live and grow for no other end but life and beauty ; and nothing that so aptly reminds me that I too have a destiny and development, whose perfection is not so much to be measured by what I *accomplish* as by *what I become*."

PRINTED BY WILLIAM BLACKWOOD AND SONS.

Catalogue

of

Messrs Blackwood & Sons'

Publications

PHILOSOPHICAL CLASSICS FOR ENGLISH READERS.

EDITED BY WILLIAM KNIGHT, LL.D.,

Professor of Moral Philosophy in the University of St Andrews.

In crown 8vo Volumes, with Portraits, price 3s. 6d.

Contents of the Series.

DESCARTES, by Professor Mahaffy, Dublin.—BUTLER, by Rev. W. Lucas Collins, M.A.—BERKELEY, by Professor Campbell Fraser.—FICHTE, by Professor Adamson, Glasgow. — KANT, by Professor Wallace, Oxford.—HAMILTON, by Professor Veitch, Glasgow.—HEGEL, by the Master of Balliol. —LEIBNIZ, by J. Theodore Merz.—VICO, by Professor Flint, Edinburgh.—HOBBES, by Professor Croom Robertson.—HUME, by the Editor. — SPINOZA, by the Very Rev. Principal Caird, Glasgow.—BACON: Part I. The Life, by Professor Nichol.—BACON: Part II. Philosophy, by the same Author.—LOCKE, by Professor Campbell Fraser.

FOREIGN CLASSICS FOR ENGLISH READERS.

EDITED BY MRS OLIPHANT.

In crown 8vo, 2s. 6d.

Contents of the Series.

DANTE, by the Editor. — VOLTAIRE, by General Sir E. B. Hamley, K.C.B. —PASCAL, by Principal Tulloch.—PETRARCH, by Henry Reeve, C.B.—GOETHE, by A. Hayward, Q.C.—MOLIÈRE, by the Editor and F. Tarver, M.A.—MONTAIGNE, by Rev. W. L. Collins, M.A.—RABELAIS, by Sir Walter Besant. — CALDERON, by E. J. Hasell. — SAINT SIMON, by Clifton W. Collins, M.A. — CERVANTES, by the Editor. — CORNEILLE AND RACINE, by Henry M. Trollope. — MADAME DE SÉVIGNÉ, by Miss Thackeray.—LA FONTAINE, AND OTHER FRENCH FABULISTS, by Rev. W. Lucas Collins, M.A.—SCHILLER, by James Sime, M.A., Author of 'Lessing, his Life and Writings.'—TASSO, by E. J. Hasell. — ROUSSEAU, by Henry Grey Graham. — ALFRED DE MUSSET, by C. F. Oliphant.

ANCIENT CLASSICS FOR ENGLISH READERS.

EDITED BY THE REV. W. LUCAS COLLINS, M.A.

Complete in 28 Vols. crown 8vo, cloth, price 2s. 6d. each. And may also be had in 14 Volumes, strongly and neatly bound, with calf or vellum back, £3, 10s.

Contents of the Series.

HOMER: THE ILIAD, by the Editor.— HOMER: THE ODYSSEY, by the Editor.— HERODOTUS, by George C. Swayne, M.A.— XENOPHON, by Sir Alexander Grant, Bart., LL.D. — EURIPIDES, by W. B. Donne.— ARISTOPHANES, by the Editor.—PLATO, by Clifton W. Collins, M.A.—LUCIAN, by the Editor. — ÆSCHYLUS, by the Right Rev. the Bishop of Colombo. — SOPHOCLES, by Clifton W. Collins, M.A. — HESIOD AND THEOGNIS, by the Rev. J. Davies, M.A.— GREEK ANTHOLOGY, by Lord Neaves.— VIRGIL, by the Editor.—HORACE, by Sir Theodore Martin, K.C.B. — JUVENAL, by Edward Walford, M.A. — PLAUTUS AND TERENCE, by the Editor.—THE COMMENTARIES OF CÆSAR, by Anthony Trollope. —TACITUS, by W. B. Donne.—CICERO, by the Editor. — PLINY'S LETTERS, by the Rev. Alfred Church, M.A., and the Rev. W. J. Brodribb, M.A. — LIVY, by the Editor.—OVID, by the Rev. A. Church, M.A.—CATULLUS, TIBULLUS, AND PROPERTIUS, by the Rev. Jas. Davies, M.A. — DEMOSTHENES, by the Rev. W. J. Brodribb, M.A.—ARISTOTLE, by Sir Alexander Grant, Bart., LL.D.—THUCYDIDES, by the Editor. — LUCRETIUS, by W. H. Mallock, M.A.—PINDAR, by the Rev. F. D. Morice, M.A.

Saturday Review.—"It is difficult to estimate too highly the value of such a series as this in giving 'English readers' an insight, exact as far as it goes, into those olden times which are so remote, and yet to many of us so close."

CATALOGUE

OF

MESSRS BLACKWOOD & SONS'
PUBLICATIONS.

ALISON.
History of Europe. By Sir ARCHIBALD ALISON, Bart., D.C.L.
1. From the Commencement of the French Revolution to the Battle of Waterloo.
LIBRARY EDITION, 14 vols., with Portraits. Demy 8vo, £10, 10s.
ANOTHER EDITION, in 20 vols. crown 8vo, £6.
PEOPLE'S EDITION, 13 vols. crown 8vo, £2, 11s.
2. Continuation to the Accession of Louis Napoleon.
LIBRARY EDITION, 8 vols. 8vo, £6, 7s. 6d.
PEOPLE'S EDITION, 8 vols. crown 8vo, 34s.

Epitome of Alison's History of Europe. Thirtieth Thousand, 7s. 6d.
Atlas to Alison's History of Europe. By A. Keith Johnston.
LIBRARY EDITION, demy 4to, £3, 3s.
PEOPLE'S EDITION, 31s. 6d.
Life of John Duke of Marlborough. With some Account of his Contemporaries, and of the War of the Succession. Third Edition. 2 vols. 8vo. Portraits and Maps, 30s.
Essays: Historical, Political, and Miscellaneous. 3 vols. demy 8vo, 45s.

ACROSS FRANCE IN A CARAVAN: BEING SOME ACCOUNT OF A JOURNEY FROM BORDEAUX TO GENOA IN THE "ESCARGOT," taken in the Winter 1889-90. By the Author of 'A Day of my Life at Eton.' With fifty Illustrations by John Wallace, after Sketches by the Author, and a Map. Cheap Edition, demy 8vo, 7s. 6d.

ACTA SANCTORUM HIBERNIÆ; Ex Codice Salmanticensi. Nunc primum integre edita opera CAROLI DE SMEDT et JOSEPHI DE BACKER, e Soc. Jesu, Hagiographorum Bollandianorum; Auctore et Sumptus Largiente JOANNE PATRICIO MARCHIONE BOTHAE. In One handsome 4to Volume, bound in half roxburghe, £2, 2s.; in paper cover, 31s. 6d.

ADOLPHUS. Some Memories of Paris. By F. ADOLPHUS. Crown 8vo, 6s.

AIKMAN.
Manures and the Principles of Manuring. By C. M. AIKMAN, D.Sc., F.R.S.E., &c., Professor of Chemistry, Glasgow Veterinary College; Examiner in Chemistry, University of Glasgow, &c. Crown 8vo, 6s. 6d.
Farmyard Manure: Its Nature, Composition, and Treatment. Crown 8vo, 1s. 6d.

AIRD. Poetical Works of Thomas Aird. Fifth Edition, with Memoir of the Author by the Rev. JARDINE WALLACE, and Portrait. Crown 8vo, 7s. 6d.

ALLARDYCE.

The City of Sunshine. By ALEXANDER ALLARDYCE, Author of
'Earlscourt,' &c. New Edition. Crown 8vo, 6s.

Balmoral : A Romance of the Queen's Country. New Edition.
Crown 8vo, 6s.

Memoir of the Honourable George Keith Elphinstone, K.B.,
Viscount Keith of Stonehaven, Marischal, Admiral of the Red. 8vo, with Portrait, Illustrations, and Maps, 21s.

ALMOND. Sermons by a Lay Head-master. By HELY HUTCH-
INSON ALMOND, M.A. Oxon., Head-Master of Loretto School. Crown 8vo, 5s.

ANCIENT CLASSICS FOR ENGLISH READERS. Edited
by Rev. W. LUCAS COLLINS, M.A. Price 2s. 6d. each. *For List of Vols., see p. 2.*

ANDERSON. Daniel in the Critics' Den. A Reply to Dean
Farrar's 'Book of Daniel.' By ROBERT ANDERSON, LL.D., Barrister-at-Law,
Assistant Commissioner of Police of the Metropolis; Author of 'The Coming
Prince,' 'Human Destiny,' &c. Post 8vo, 4s. 6d.

AYTOUN.

Lays of the Scottish Cavaliers, and other Poems. By W.
EDMONDSTOUNE AYTOUN, D.C.L., Professor of Rhetoric and Belles-Lettres in the
University of Edinburgh. New Edition. Fcap. 8vo, 3s. 6d.
ANOTHER EDITION. Fcap. 8vo, 7s. 6d.
CHEAP EDITION. 1s. Cloth, 1s. 3d.

An Illustrated Edition of the Lays of the Scottish Cavaliers.
From designs by Sir NOEL PATON. Cheaper Edition. Small 4to, 10s. 6d.

Bothwell : a Poem. Third Edition. Fcap., 7s. 6d.

Poems and Ballads of Goethe. Translated by Professor
AYTOUN and Sir THEODORE MARTIN, K.C.B. Third Edition. Fcap., 6s.

The Ballads of Scotland. Edited by Professor AYTOUN.
Fourth Edition. 2 vols. fcap. 8vo, 12s.

Memoir of William E. Aytoun, D.C.L. By Sir THEODORE
MARTIN, K.C.B. With Portrait. Post 8vo, 12s.

BACH.

On Musical Education and Vocal Culture. By ALBERT B.
BACH. Fourth Edition. 8vo, 7s. 6d.

The Principles of Singing. A Practical Guide for Vocalists
and Teachers. With Course of Vocal Exercises. Second Edition. With Portrait
of the Author. Crown 8vo, 6s.

The Art Ballad : Loewe and Schubert. With Musical Illustrations. With a Portrait of LOEWE. Third Edition. Small 4to, 5s.

BEDFORD & COLLINS. Annals of the Free Foresters, from
1856 to the Present Day. By W. K. R. BEDFORD, W. E. W. COLLINS, and other
Contributors. With 55 Portraits and 59 other Illustrations. Demy 8vo, 21s. *net.*

BELLAIRS. Gossips with Girls and Maidens, Betrothed and
Free. By LADY BELLAIRS. New Edition. Crown 8vo, 3s. 6d. Cloth, extra
gilt edges, 5s.

BELLESHEIM. History of the Catholic Church of Scotland.
From the Introduction of Christianity to the Present Day. By ALPHONS BEL-
LESHEIM, D.D., Canon of Aix-la-Chapelle. Translated, with Notes and Additions,
by D. OSWALD HUNTER BLAIR, O.S.B., Monk of Fort Augustus. Cheap Edition.
Complete in 4 vols. demy 8vo, with Maps. Price 21s. net.

BENTINCK. Racing Life of Lord George Cavendish Bentinck,
M.P., and other Reminiscences. By JOHN KENT, Private Trainer to the Good-
wood Stable. Edited by the Hon. FRANCIS LAWLEY. With Twenty-three full-
page Plates, and Facsimile Letter. Third Edition. Demy 8vo, 25s.

BESANT. The Revolt of Man. By Sir WALTER BESANT.
Tenth Edition. Crown 8vo, 3s. 6d.

BEVERIDGE.
Culross and Tulliallan ; or, Perthshire on Forth. Its History
and Antiquities. With Elucidations of Scottish Life and Character from the
Burgh and Kirk-Session Records of that District. By DAVID BEVERIDGE. 2 vols.
8vo, with Illustrations, 42s.
Between the Ochils and the Forth ; or, From Stirling Bridge
to Aberdour. Crown 8vo, 6s.

BICKERDYKE. A Banished Beauty. By JOHN BICKERDYKE,
Author of 'Days in Thule, with Rod, Gun, and Camera,' 'The Book of the All-
Round Angler,' 'Curiosities of Ale and Beer,' &c. With Illustrations. Crown
8vo, 6s.

BIRCH.
Examples of Stables, Hunting-Boxes, Kennels, Racing Estab-
lishments, &c. By JOHN BIRCH, Architect, Author of 'Country Architecture,'
&c. With 30 Plates. Royal 8vo, 7s.
Examples of Labourers' Cottages, &c. With Plans for Im-
proving the Dwellings of the Poor in Large Towns. With 34 Plates. Royal 8vo, 7s.
Picturesque Lodges. A Series of Designs for Gate Lodges,
Park Entrances, Keepers', Gardeners', Bailiffs', Grooms', Upper and Under Servants' Lodges, and other Rural Residences. With 16 Plates. 4to, 12s. 6d.

BLACK. Heligoland and the Islands of the North Sea. By
WILLIAM GEORGE BLACK. Crown 8vo, 4s.

BLACKIE.
Lays and Legends of Ancient Greece. By JOHN STUART
BLACKIE, Emeritus Professor of Greek in the University of Edinburgh. Second
Edition. Fcap. 8vo, 5s.
The Wisdom of Goethe. Fcap. 8vo. Cloth, extra gilt, 6s.
Scottish Song : Its Wealth, Wisdom, and Social Significance.
Crown 8vo. With Music. 7s. 6d.
A Song of Heroes. Crown 8vo, 6s.
John Stuart Blackie : A Biography. By ANNA M. STODDART.
With 3 Plates. Third Edition. 2 vols. demy 8vo, 21s.
POPULAR EDITION. With Portrait. Crown 8vo, 6s.

BLACKMORE. The Maid of Sker. By R. D. BLACKMORE,
Author of 'Lorna Doone,' &c. New Edition. Crown 8vo, 6s. Cheaper Edition. Crown 8vo, 3s. 6d.

BLACKWOOD.
Blackwood's Magazine, from Commencement in 1817 to August
1896. Nos. 1 to 970, forming 159 Volumes.
Index to Blackwood's Magazine. Vols. 1 to 50. 8vo, 15s.
Tales from Blackwood. First Series. Price One Shilling each,
in Paper Cover. Sold separately at all Railway Bookstalls.
They may also be had bound in 12 vols., cloth, 18s. Half calf, richly gilt, 30s.
Or the 12 vols. in 6, roxburghe, 21s. Half red morocco, 28s.
Tales from Blackwood. Second Series. Complete in Twenty-
four Shilling Parts. Handsomely bound in 12 vols., cloth, 30s. In leather back,
roxburghe style, 37s. 6d. Half calf, gilt, 52s. 6d. Half morocco, 55s.
Tales from Blackwood. Third Series. Complete in Twelve
Shilling Parts. Handsomely bound in 6 vols., cloth, 15s.; and in 12 vols., cloth,
18s. The 6 vols. in roxburghe, 21s. Half calf, 25s. Half morocco, 28s.
Travel, Adventure, and Sport. From 'Blackwood's Magazine.'
Uniform with 'Tales from Blackwood.' In Twelve Parts, each price 1s. Handsomely bound in 6 vols., cloth, 15s. And in half calf, 25s.

BLACKWOOD.

New Educational Series. *See separate Catalogue.*
New Uniform Series of Novels (Copyright).
Crown 8vo, cloth.   Price 3s. 6d. each.   Now ready:—

THE MAID OF SKER. By R. D. Blackmore.
WENDERHOLME. By P. G. Hamerton.
THE STORY OF MARGRÉDEL. By D. Storrar Meldrum.
MISS MARJORIBANKS. By Mrs Oliphant.
THE PERPETUAL CURATE, and THE RECTOR. By the Same.
SALEM CHAPEL, and THE DOCTOR'S FAMILY. By the Same.
A SENSITIVE PLANT. By E. D. Gerard.
LADY LEE'S WIDOWHOOD. By General Sir E. B. Hamley.
KATIE STEWART, and other Stories. By Mrs Oliphant.
VALENTINE AND HIS BROTHER. By the Same.
SONS AND DAUGHTERS. By the Same.
MARMORNE. By P. G. Hamerton.

REATA. By E. D. Gerard.
BEGGAR MY NEIGHBOUR. By the Same.
THE WATERS OF HERCULES. By the Same.
FAIR TO SEE. By L. W. M. Lockhart.
MINE IS THINE. By the Same.
DOUBLES AND QUITS. By the Same.
ALTIORA PETO. By Laurence Oliphant.
PICCADILLY. By the Same. With Illustrations.
THE REVOLT OF MAN. By Walter Besant.
LADY BABY. By D. Gerard.
THE BLACKSMITH OF VOE. By Paul Cushing.
THE DILEMMA. By the Author of 'The Battle of Dorking.'
MY TRIVIAL LIFE AND MISFORTUNE. By A Plain Woman.
POOR NELLIE. By the Same.

Others in preparation.

Standard Novels.   Uniform in size and binding.   Each complete in one Volume.

FLORIN SERIES, Illustrated Boards. Bound in Cloth, 2s. 6d.

TOM CRINGLE'S LOG. By Michael Scott.
THE CRUISE OF THE MIDGE. By the Same.
CYRIL THORNTON. By Captain Hamilton.
ANNALS OF THE PARISH. By John Galt.
THE PROVOST, &c. By the Same.
SIR ANDREW WYLIE. By the Same.
THE ENTAIL. By the Same.
MISS MOLLY. By Beatrice May Butt.
REGINALD DALTON. By J. G. Lockhart.

PEN OWEN. By Dean Hook.
ADAM BLAIR. By J. G. Lockhart.
LADY LEE'S WIDOWHOOD. By General Sir E. B. Hamley.
SALEM CHAPEL. By Mrs Oliphant.
THE PERPETUAL CURATE. By the Same.
MISS MARJORIBANKS. By the Same.
JOHN: A Love Story. By the Same.

SHILLING SERIES, Illustrated Cover. Bound in Cloth, 1s. 6d.

THE RECTOR, and THE DOCTOR'S FAMILY. By Mrs Oliphant.
THE LIFE OF MANSIE WAUCH. By D. M. Moir.
PENINSULAR SCENES AND SKETCHES. By F. Hardman.

SIR FRIZZLE PUMPKIN, NIGHTS AT MESS, &c.
THE SUBALTERN.
LIFE IN THE FAR WEST. By G. F. Ruxton.
VALERIUS: A Roman Story. By J. G. Lockhart.

BON GAULTIER'S BOOK OF BALLADS. Fifteenth Edition. With Illustrations by Doyle, Leech, and Crowquill. Fcap. 8vo, 5s.

BRADDON. Thirty Years of Shikar. By Sir EDWARD BRADDON, K.C.M.G. With Illustrations by G. D. Giles, and Map of Oudh Forest Tracts and Nepal Terai. Demy 8vo, 18s.

BROUGHAM. Memoirs of the Life and Times of Henry Lord Brougham. Written by HIMSELF. 3 vols. 8vo, £2, 8s. The Volumes are sold separately, price 16s. each.

BROWN. The Forester: A Practical Treatise on the Planting and Tending of Forest-trees and the General Management of Woodlands. By JAMES BROWN, LL.D. Sixth Edition, Enlarged. Edited by JOHN NISBET, D.Œc., Author of 'British Forest Trees,' &c. In 2 vols. royal 8vo, with 350 Illustrations, 42s. net.

BROWN. Stray Sport. By J. MORAY BROWN, Author of 'Shikar Sketches,' 'Powder, Spur, and Spear,' 'The Days when we went Hog-Hunting.' 2 vols. post 8vo, with Fifty Illustrations, 21s.

BROWN. A Manual of Botany, Anatomical and Physiological. For the Use of Students. By ROBERT BROWN, M.A., Ph.D. Crown 8vo, with numerous Illustrations, 12s. 6d.

BRUCE.

In Clover and Heather. Poems by WALLACE BRUCE. New and Enlarged Edition. Crown 8vo, 3s. 6d.
A limited number of Copies of the First Edition, on large hand-made paper, 12s. 6d.

Here's a Hand. Addresses and Poems. Crown 8vo, 5s.
Large Paper Edition, limited to 100 copies, price 21s.

BUCHAN. Introductory Text-Book of Meteorology. By ALEXANDER BUCHAN, LL.D., F.R.S.E., Secretary of the Scottish Meteorological Society, &c. New Edition. Crown 8vo, with Coloured Charts and Engravings.
[*In preparation.*

BURBIDGE.

Domestic Floriculture, Window Gardening, and Floral Decorations. Being Practical Directions for the Propagation, Culture, and Arrangement of Plants and Flowers as Domestic Ornaments. By F. W. BURBIDGE. Second Edition. Crown 8vo, with numerous Illustrations, 7s. 6d.

Cultivated Plants: Their Propagation and Improvement. Including Natural and Artificial Hybridisation, Raising from Seed, Cuttings, and Layers, Grafting and Budding, as applied to the Families and Genera in Cultivation. Crown 8vo, with numerous Illustrations, 12s. 6d.

BURGESS. The Viking Path: A Tale of the White Christ. By J. J. HALDANE BURGESS, Author of 'Rasmie's Büddie,' 'Shetland Sketches,' &c. Crown 8vo, 6s.

BURKE. The Flowering of the Almond Tree, and other Poems. By CHRISTIAN BURKE. Pott 4to, 5s.

BURROWS.

Commentaries on the History of England, from the Earliest Times to 1865. By MONTAGU BURROWS, Chichele Professor of Modern History in the University of Oxford; Captain R.N.; F.S.A., &c.; "Officier de l'Instruction Publique," France. Crown 8vo, 7s. 6d.

The History of the Foreign Policy of Great Britain. Demy 8vo, 12s.

BURTON.

The History of Scotland: From Agricola's Invasion to the Extinction of the last Jacobite Insurrection. By JOHN HILL BURTON, D.C.L., Historiographer-Royal for Scotland. New and Enlarged Edition, 8 vols., and Index. Crown 8vo, £3, 3s.

History of the British Empire during the Reign of Queen Anne. In 3 vols. 8vo. 36s.

The Scot Abroad. Third Edition. Crown 8vo, 10s. 6d.

The Book-Hunter. New Edition. With Portrait. Crown 8vo, 7s. 6d.

BUTCHER. The Fortunes of Armenosa. A Historical Romance of Memphis and Old Cairo. By the Very Rev. Dean BUTCHER, D.D., F.S.A., Chaplain at Cairo. Crown 8vo, 6s.

BUTE. The Altus of St Columba. With a Prose Paraphrase and Notes. In paper cover, 2s. 6d.

BUTT.

Theatricals: An Interlude. By BEATRICE MAY BUTT. Crown 8vo, 6s.

Miss Molly. Cheap Edition, 2s.

Eugenie. Crown 8vo, 6s. 6d.

Elizabeth, and other Sketches. Crown 8vo, 6s.

Delicia. New Edition. Crown 8vo, 2s. 6d.

CAIRD. Sermons. By JOHN CAIRD, D.D., Principal of the University of Glasgow. Seventeenth Thousand. Fcap. 8vo, 5s.

CALDWELL. Schopenhauer's System in its Philosophical Significance (the Shaw Fellowship Lectures, 1893). By WILLIAM CALDWELL, M.A., D.Sc., Professor of Moral and Social Philosophy, Northwestern University, U.S.A.; formerly Assistant to the Professor of Logic and Metaphysics, Edin., and Examiner in Philosophy in the University of St Andrews. Demy 8vo, 10s. 6d. net.

CALLWELL. The Effect of Maritime Command on Land Campaigns since Waterloo. By Major C. E. CALLWELL, R.A. With Plans. Post 8vo, 6s. *net.*

CAMPBELL. Sermons Preached before the Queen at Balmoral. By the Rev. A. A. CAMPBELL, Minister of Crathie. Published by Command of Her Majesty. Crown 8vo, 4s. 6d.

CAMPBELL. Records of Argyll. Legends, Traditions, and Recollections of Argyllshire Highlanders, collected chiefly from the Gaelic. With Notes on the Antiquity of the Dress, Clan Colours, or Tartans of the Highlanders. By Lord ARCHIBALD CAMPBELL. Illustrated with Nineteen full-page Etchings. 4to, printed on hand-made paper, £3, 3s.

CAMPBELL. Critical Studies in St Luke's Gospel : Its Demonology and Ebionitism. By COLIN CAMPBELL, D.D., Minister of the Parish of Dundee, formerly Scholar and Fellow of Glasgow University. Author of the 'Three First Gospels in Greek, arranged in parallel columns.' Post 8vo, 7s. 6d.

CANTON. A Lost Epic, and other Poems. By WILLIAM CANTON. Crown 8vo, 5s.

CARSTAIRS.
Human Nature in Rural India. By R. CARSTAIRS. Crown 8vo, 6s.
British Work in India. Crown 8vo, 6s.

CAUVIN. A Treasury of the English and German Languages. Compiled from the best Authors and Lexicographers in both Languages. By JOSEPH CAUVIN, LL.D. and Ph.D., of the University of Göttingen, &c. Crown 8vo, 7s. 6d.

CHARTERIS. Canonicity; or, Early Testimonies to the Existence and Use of the Books of the New Testament. Based on Kirchhoffer's 'Quellensammlung.' Edited by A. H. CHARTERIS, D.D., Professor of Biblical Criticism in the University of Edinburgh. [*New Edition in preparation.*

CHENNELLS. Recollections of an Egyptian Princess. By her English Governess (Miss E. CHENNELLS). Being a Record of Five Years' Residence at the Court of Ismael Pasha, Khédive. Second Edition. With Three Portraits. Post 8vo, 7s. 6d.

CHESNEY. The Dilemma. By General Sir GEORGE CHESNEY, K.C.B., M.P., Author of 'The Battle of Dorking,' &c. New Edition. Crown 8vo, 3s. 6d.

CHRISTISON. Life of Sir Robert Christison, Bart., M.D., D.C.L. Oxon., Professor of Medical Jurisprudence in the University of Edinburgh. Edited by his SONS. In 2 vols. 8vo. Vol. I.—Autobiography. 16s. Vol. II.—Memoirs. 16s.

CHURCH. Chapters in an Adventurous Life. Sir Richard Church in Italy and Greece. By E. M. CHURCH. With Photogravure Portrait. Demy 8vo, 10s. 6d.

CHURCH SERVICE SOCIETY.
A Book of Common Order : being Forms of Worship issued by the Church Service Society. Seventh Edition, carefully revised. In 1 vol. crown 8vo, cloth, 3s. 6d.; French morocco, 5s. Also in 2 vols. crown 8vo, cloth, 4s.; French morocco, 6s. 6d.
Daily Offices for Morning and Evening Prayer throughout the Week. Crown 8vo, 3s. 6d.
Order of Divine Service for Children. Issued by the Church Service Society. With Scottish Hymnal. Cloth, 3d.

CLOUSTON. Popular Tales and Fictions: their Migrations and Transformations. By W. A. CLOUSTON, Editor of 'Arabian Poetry for English Readers,' &c. 2 vols. post 8vo, roxburghe binding, 25s.

COCHRAN. A Handy Text-Book of Military Law. Compiled chiefly to assist Officers preparing for Examination; also for all Officers of the Regular and Auxiliary Forces. Comprising also a Synopsis of part of the Army Act. By Major F. COCHRAN, Hampshire Regiment Garrison Instructor, North British District. Crown 8vo, 7s. 6d.

COLQUHOUN. The Moor and the Loch. Containing Minute Instructions in all Highland Sports, with Wanderings over Crag and Corrie, Flood and Fell. By JOHN COLQUHOUN. Cheap Edition. With Illustrations. Demy 8vo, 10s. 6d.

COLVILE. Round the Black Man's Garden. By Lady Z. COLVILE, F.R.G.S. With 2 Maps and 50 Illustrations from Drawings by the Author and from Photographs. Demy 8vo, 16s.

CONDER. The Bible and the East. By Lieut.-Col. C. R. CONDER, R.E., LL.D., D.C.L., M.R.A.S., Author of 'Tent Work in Palestine,' &c. With Illustrations and a Map. Crown 8vo, 5s.

CONSTITUTION AND LAW OF THE CHURCH OF SCOTLAND. With an Introductory Note by the late Principal Tulloch. New Edition, Revised and Enlarged. Crown 8vo, 3s. 6d.

COTTERILL. Suggested Reforms in Public Schools. By C. C. COTTERILL, M.A. Crown 8vo, 3s. 6d.

COUNTY HISTORIES OF SCOTLAND. In demy 8vo volumes of about 350 pp. each. With 2 Maps. Price 7s. 6d. net.

Fife and Kinross. By ÆNEAS J. G. MACKAY, LL.D., Sheriff of these Counties.

Dumfries and Galloway. By Sir HERBERT MAXWELL, Bart., M.P. *[Others in preparation.*

CRANSTOUN.

The Elegies of Albius Tibullus. Translated into English Verse, with Life of the Poet, and Illustrative Notes. By JAMES CRANSTOUN, LL.D., Author of a Translation of 'Catullus.' Crown 8vo, 6s. 6d.

The Elegies of Sextus Propertius. Translated into English Verse, with Life of the Poet, and Illustrative Notes. Crown 8vo, 7s. 6d.

CRAWFORD. Saracinesca. By F. MARION CRAWFORD, Author of 'Mr Isaacs,' &c., &c. Eighth Edition. Crown 8vo, 6s.

CRAWFORD.

The Doctrine of Holy Scripture respecting the Atonement. By the late THOMAS J. CRAWFORD, D.D., Professor of Divinity in the University of Edinburgh. Fifth Edition. 8vo, 12s.

The Fatherhood of God, Considered in its General and Special Aspects. Third Edition, Revised and Enlarged. 8vo, 9s.

The Preaching of the Cross, and other Sermons. 8vo, 7s. 6d.

The Mysteries of Christianity. Crown 8vo, 7s. 6d.

CROSS. Impressions of Dante, and of the New World; with a Few Words on Bimetallism. By J. W. CROSS, Editor of 'George Eliot's Life, as related in her Letters and Journals.' Post 8vo, 6s.

CUMBERLAND. Sport on the Pamirs and Turkistan Steppes. By Major C. S. CUMBERLAND. With Map and Frontispiece. Demy 8vo, 10s. 6d.

CURSE OF INTELLECT. Third Edition. Fcap. 8vo, 2s. 6d. net.

CUSHING. The Blacksmith of Voe. By PAUL CUSHING, Author of 'The Bull i' th' Thorn,' 'Cut with his own Diamond.' Cheap Edition. Crown 8vo, 3s. 6d.

DAVIES.

Norfolk Broads and Rivers; or, The Waterways, Lagoons, and Decoys of East Anglia. By G. CHRISTOPHER DAVIES. Illustrated with Seven full-page Plates. New and Cheaper Edition. Crown 8vo, 6s.

Our Home in Aveyron. Sketches of Peasant Life in Aveyron and the Lot. By G. CHRISTOPHER DAVIES and Mrs BROUGHALL. Illustrated with full-page Illustrations. 8vo, 15s. Cheap Edition, 7s. 6d.

DE LA WARR. An Eastern Cruise in the 'Edeline.' By the Countess DE LA WARR. In Illustrated Cover. 2s.

DESCARTES. The Method, Meditations, and Principles of Philosophy of Descartes. Translated from the Original French and Latin. With a New Introductory Essay, Historical and Critical, on the Cartesian Philosophy. By Professor VEITCH, LL.D., Glasgow University. Tenth Edition. 6s. 6d.

DOGS, OUR DOMESTICATED : Their Treatment in reference to Food, Diseases, Habits, Punishment, Accomplishments. By 'MAGENTA.' Crown 8vo, 2s. 6d.

DOUGLAS.

The Ethics of John Stuart Mill. By CHARLES DOUGLAS, M.A., D.Sc., Lecturer in Moral Philosophy, and Assistant to the Professor of Moral Philosophy in the University of Edinburgh. Crown 8vo, 7s. 6d. *net.*

John Stuart Mill: A Study of his Philosophy. Crown 8vo, 4s. 6d. net.

DOUGLAS. Chinese Stories. By ROBERT K. DOUGLAS. With numerous Illustrations by Parkinson, Forestier, and others. New and Cheaper Edition. Small demy 8vo, 5s.

DOUGLAS. Iras: A Mystery. By THEO. DOUGLAS, Author of 'A Bride Elect.' Crown 8vo, 3s. 6d.

DU CANE. The Odyssey of Homer, Books I.-XII. Translated into English Verse. By Sir CHARLES DU CANE, K.C.M.G. 8vo, 10s. 6d.

DUDGEON. History of the Edinburgh or Queen's Regiment Light Infantry Militia, now 3rd Battalion The Royal Scots; with an Account of the Origin and Progress of the Militia, and a Brief Sketch of the Old Royal Scots. By Major R. C. DUDGEON, Adjutant 3rd Battalion the Royal Scots. Post 8vo, with Illustrations, 10s. 6d.

DUNSMORE. Manual of the Law of Scotland as to the Relations between Agricultural Tenants and the Landlords, Servants, Merchants, and Bowers. By W. DUNSMORE. 8vo, 7s. 6d.

ELIOT.

George Eliot's Life, Related in Her Letters and Journals. Arranged and Edited by her husband, J. W. CROSS. With Portrait and other Illustrations. Third Edition. 3 vols. post 8vo, 42s.

George Eliot's Life. With Portrait and other Illustrations. New Edition, in one volume. Crown 8vo, 7s. 6d.

Works of George Eliot (Standard Edition). 21 volumes, crown 8vo. In buckram cloth, gilt top, 2s. 6d. per vol. ; or in roxburghe binding, 3s. 6d. per vol.
ADAM BEDE. 2 vols.—THE MILL ON THE FLOSS. 2 vols.—FELIX HOLT, THE RADICAL. 2 vols.—ROMOLA. 2 vols.—SCENES OF CLERICAL LIFE. 2 vols.— MIDDLEMARCH. 3 vols.—DANIEL DERONDA. 3 vols.—SILAS MARNER. 1 vol. —JUBAL. 1 vol.—THE SPANISH GIPSY. 1 vol.—ESSAYS. 1 vol.—THEOPHRASTUS SUCH. 1 vol.

Life and Works of George Eliot (Cabinet Edition). 24 volumes, crown 8vo, price £6. Also to be had handsomely bound in half and full calf. The Volumes are sold separately, bound in cloth, price 5s. each.

ELIOT.
Novels by George Eliot. Cheap Edition.
Adam Bede. Illustrated. 3s. 6d., cloth.—The Mill on the Floss. Illustrated. 3s. 6d., cloth.—Scenes of Clerical Life. Illustrated. 3s., cloth.—Silas Marner: the Weaver of Raveloe. Illustrated. 2s. 6d., cloth.—Felix Holt, the Radical. Illustrated. 3s. 6d., cloth.—Romola. With Vignette. 3s. 6d., cloth.
Middlemarch. Crown 8vo, 7s. 6d.
Daniel Deronda. Crown 8vo, 7s. 6d.
Essays. New Edition. Crown 8vo, 5s.
Impressions of Theophrastus Such. New Edition. Crown 8vo, 5s.
The Spanish Gypsy. New Edition. Crown 8vo, 5s.
The Legend of Jubal, and other Poems, Old and New. New Edition. Crown 8vo, 5s.
Wise, Witty, and Tender Sayings, in Prose and Verse. Selected from the Works of GEORGE ELIOT. New Edition. Fcap. 8vo, 3s. 6d.
ENGLISH CHURCH AND THE ROMISH SCHISM. Crown 8vo, 2s. 6d.
ESSAYS ON SOCIAL SUBJECTS. Originally published in the 'Saturday Review.' New Edition. First and Second Series. 2 vols. crown 8vo, 6s. each.

FAITHS OF THE WORLD, The. A Concise History of the Great Religious Systems of the World. By various Authors. Crown 8vo, 5s.
FALKNER. The Lost Stradivarius. By J. MEADE FALKNER. Second Edition. Crown 8vo, 6s.
FERGUSON. Sir Samuel Ferguson in the Ireland of his Day. By LADY FERGUSON, Author of 'The Irish before the Conquest,' 'Life of William Reeves, D.D., Lord Bishop of Down, Connor, and Drumore,' &c., &c. With Two Portraits. 2 vols. post 8vo, 21s.
FERRIER.
Philosophical Works of the late James F. Ferrier, B.A. Oxon., Professor of Moral Philosophy and Political Economy, St Andrews. New Edition. Edited by Sir ALEXANDER GRANT, Bart., D.C.L., and Professor LUSHINGTON. 3 vols. crown 8vo, 34s. 6d.
Institutes of Metaphysic. Third Edition. 10s. 6d.
Lectures on the Early Greek Philosophy. 4th Edition. 10s. 6d.
Philosophical Remains, including the Lectures on Early Greek Philosophy. New Edition. 2 vols. 24s.
FLINT.
Historical Philosophy in France and French Belgium and Switzerland. By ROBERT FLINT, Corresponding Member of the Institute of France, Hon. Member of the Royal Society of Palermo, Professor in the University of Edinburgh, &c. 8vo, 21s.
Agnosticism. Being the Croall Lecture for 1887-88.
[In the press.
Theism. Being the Baird Lecture for 1876. Ninth Edition, Revised. Crown 8vo, 7s. 6d.
Anti-Theistic Theories. Being the Baird Lecture for 1877. Fifth Edition. Crown 8vo, 10s. 6d.
FOREIGN CLASSICS FOR ENGLISH READERS. Edited by Mrs OLIPHANT. Price 2s. 6d. *For List of Volumes, see page 2.*
FOSTER. The Fallen City, and other Poems. By WILL FOSTER. Crown 8vo, 6s.

FRANCILLON.   Gods and Heroes ; or, The Kingdom of Jupiter.
By R. E. FRANCILLON.   With 8 Illustrations.   Crown 8vo, 5s.

FRANCIS.   Among the Untrodden Ways.   By M. E. FRANCIS
(Mrs Francis Blundell), Author of 'In a North Country Village,' 'A Daughter of
the Soil,' 'Frieze and Fustian,' &c.   Crown 8vo, 3s. 6d.

FRASER.
Philosophy of Theism.   Being the Gifford Lectures delivered
before the University of Edinburgh in 1894-95.   First Series.   By ALEXANDER
CAMPBELL FRASER, D.C.L. Oxford ; Emeritus Professor of Logic and Metaphysics in the University of Edinburgh.   Post 8vo, 7s. 6d. net.

Philosophy of Theism.   Being the Gifford Lectures delivered
before the University of Edinburgh in 1895-96.   Second Series.   Post 8vo,
7s. 6d. *net*.

FRASER.   St Mary's of Old Montrose : A History of the Parish
of Maryton.   By the Rev. WILLIAM RUXTON FRASER, M.A., F.S.A. Scot.,
Emeritus Minister of Maryton ; Author of 'History of the Parish and Burgh of
Laurencekirk.''   Crown 8vo, 3s. 6d.

FULLARTON.
Merlin : A Dramatic Poem.   By RALPH MACLEOD FULLAR-
TON.   Crown 8vo, 5s.

Tanhäuser.   Crown 8vo, 6s.

Lallan Sangs and German Lyrics.   Crown 8vo, 5s.

GALT.
Novels by JOHN GALT.   With General Introduction and
Prefatory Notes by S. R. CROCKETT.   The Text Revised and Edited by D.
STORRAR MELDRUM, Author of 'The Story of Margrédel.'   With Photogravure
Illustrations from Drawings by John Wallace.   Fcap. 8vo, 3s. net each vol.

ANNALS OF THE PARISH, and THE AYRSHIRE LEGATEES.   2 vols.—SIR ANDREW
WYLIE.   2 vols.—THE ENTAIL ; or, The Lairds of Grippy.   2 vols.—THE PRO-
VOST, and THE LAST OF THE LAIRDS.   2 vols.

See also STANDARD NOVELS, p. 6.

GENERAL ASSEMBLY OF THE CHURCH OF SCOTLAND.
Scottish Hymnal, With Appendix Incorporated.   Published
for use in Churches by Authority of the General Assembly.   1. Large type,
cloth, red edges, 2s. 6d.; French morocco, 4s.   2. Bourgeois type, limp cloth, 1s.;
French morocco, 2s.   3. Nonpareil type, cloth, red edges, 6d.; French morocco,
1s. 4d.   4. Paper covers, 3d.   5. Sunday-School Edition, paper covers, 1d.,
cloth, 2d.   No. 1, bound with the Psalms and Paraphrases, French morocco, 8s.
No. 2, bound with the Psalms and Paraphrases, cloth, 2s.; French morocco, 3s.

Prayers for Social and Family Worship.   Prepared by a
Special Committee of the General Assembly of the Church of Scotland.   Entirely
New Edition, Revised and Enlarged.   Fcap. 8vo, red edges, 2s.

Prayers for Family Worship.   A Selection of Four Weeks'
Prayers.   New Edition.   Authorised by the General Assembly of the Church of
Scotland.   Fcap. 8vo, red edges, 1s. 6d.

One Hundred Prayers.   Prepared by the Committee on Aids
to Devotion.   16mo, cloth limp, 6d.

Morning and Evening Prayers for Affixing to Bibles.   Prepared
by the Committee on Aids to Devotion.   1d. for 6, or 1s. per 100.

GERARD.
Reata : What's in a Name.   By E. D. GERARD.   Cheap
Edition.   Crown 8vo, 3s. 6d.

Beggar my Neighbour.   Cheap Edition.   Crown 8vo, 3s. 6d.

The Waters of Hercules.   Cheap Edition.   Crown 8vo, 3s. 6d.

A Sensitive Plant.   Crown 8vo, 3s. 6d.

GERARD.
A Foreigner. An Anglo-German Study. By E. GERARD.
Crown 8vo, 6s.
The Land beyond the Forest. Facts, Figures, and Fancies
from Transylvania. With Maps and Illustrations. 2 vols. post 8vo, 25s.
Bis : Some Tales Retold. Crown 8vo, 6s.
A Secret Mission. 2 vols. crown 8vo, 17s.
GERARD.
The Wrong Man. By DOROTHEA GERARD. Second Edition.
Crown 8vo, 6s.
Lady Baby. Cheap Edition. Crown 8vo, 3s. 6d.
Recha. Second Edition. Crown 8vo, 6s.
The Rich Miss Riddell. Second Edition. Crown 8vo, 6s.
GERARD. Stonyhurst Latin Grammar. By Rev. JOHN GERARD.
Second Edition. Fcap. 8vo, 3s.
GILL.
Free Trade : an Inquiry into the Nature of its Operation.
By RICHARD GILL. Crown 8vo, 7s. 6d.
Free Trade under Protection. Crown 8vo, 7s. 6d.
GORDON CUMMING.
At Home in Fiji. By C. F. GORDON CUMMING. Fourth
Edition, post 8vo. With Illustrations and Map. 7s. 6d.
A Lady's Cruise in a French Man-of-War. New and Cheaper
Edition. 8vo. With Illustrations and Map. 12s. 6d.
Fire-Fountains. The Kingdom of Hawaii : Its Volcanoes,
and the History of its Missions. With Map and Illustrations. 2 vols. 8vo, 25s.
Wanderings in China. New and Cheaper Edition. 8vo, with
Illustrations, 10s.
Granite Crags : The Yŏ-semité Region of California. Illus-
trated with 8 Engravings. New and Cheaper Edition. 8vo, 8s. 6d.
GRAHAM. Manual of the Elections (Scot.) (Corrupt and Illegal
Practices) Act, 1890. With Analysis, Relative Act of Sederunt, Appendix con-
taining the Corrupt Practices Acts of 1883 and 1885, and Copious Index. By J.
EDWARD GRAHAM, Advocate. 8vo, 4s. 6d.
GRAND.
A Domestic Experiment. By SARAH GRAND, Author of
'The Heavenly Twins,' 'Ideala : A Study from Life.' Crown 8vo, 6s.
Singularly Deluded. Crown 8vo, 6s.
GRANT. Bush-Life in Queensland. By A. C. GRANT. New
Edition. Crown 8vo, 6s.
GRANT. Life of Sir Hope Grant. With Selections from his
Correspondence. Edited by HENRY KNOLLYS, Colonel (H.P.) Royal Artillery,
his former A.D.C., Editor of 'Incidents in the Sepoy War ;' Author of 'Sketches
of Life in Japan,' &c. With Portraits of Sir Hope Grant and other Illus-
trations. Maps and Plans. 2 vols. demy 8vo, 21s.
GRIER.
In Furthest Ind. The Narrative of Mr EDWARD CARLYON of
Ellswether, in the County of Northampton, and late of the Honourable East India
Company's Service, Gentleman. Wrote by his own hand in the year of grace 1697.
Edited, with a few Explanatory Notes, by SYDNEY C. GRIER. Post 8vo, 6s.
His Excellency's English Governess. Crown 8vo, 6s.
An Uncrowned King : A Romance of High Politics. Crown
8vo, 6s.
GUTHRIE - SMITH. Crispus : A Drama. By H. GUTHRIE-
SMITH. Fcap. 4to, 5s.

HAGGARD. Under Crescent and Star. By Lieut.-Col. ANDREW HAGGARD, D.S.O., Author of 'Dodo and I,' 'Tempest Torn,' &c. With a Portrait. Second Edition. Crown 8vo, 6s.

HALDANE. Subtropical Cultivations and Climates. A Handy Book for Planters, Colonists, and Settlers. By R. C. HALDANE. Post 8vo, 9s.

HAMERTON.
Wenderholme: A Story of Lancashire and Yorkshire Life. By P. G. HAMERTON, Author of 'A Painter's Camp.' New Edition. Crown 8vo, 3s. 6d.
Marmorne. New Edition. Crown 8vo, 3s. 6d.

HAMILTON.
Lectures on Metaphysics. By Sir WILLIAM HAMILTON, Bart., Professor of Logic and Metaphysics in the University of Edinburgh. Edited by the Rev. H. L. MANSEL, B.D., LL.D., Dean of St Paul's; and JOHN VEITCH, M.A., LL.D., Professor of Logic and Rhetoric, Glasgow. Seventh Edition. 2 vols. 8vo, 24s.
Lectures on Logic. Edited by the SAME. Third Edition, Revised. 2 vols., 24s.
Discussions on Philosophy and Literature, Education and University Reform. Third Edition. 8vo, 21s.
Memoir of Sir William Hamilton, Bart., Professor of Logic and Metaphysics in the University of Edinburgh. By Professor VEITCH, of the University of Glasgow. 8vo, with Portrait, 18s.
Sir William Hamilton: The Man and his Philosophy. Two Lectures delivered before the Edinburgh Philosophical Institution, January and February 1883. By Professor VEITCH. Crown 8vo, 2s.

HAMLEY.
The Operations of War Explained and Illustrated. By General Sir EDWARD BRUCE HAMLEY, K.C.B., K.C.M.G. Fifth Edition, Revised throughout. 4to, with numerous Illustrations, 30s.
National Defence; Articles and Speeches. Post 8vo, 6s.
Shakespeare's Funeral, and other Papers. Post 8vo, 7s. 6d.
Thomas Carlyle: An Essay. Second Edition. Crown 8vo, 2s. 6d.
On Outposts. Second Edition. 8vo, 2s.
Wellington's Career; A Military and Political Summary. Crown 8vo, 2s.
Lady Lee's Widowhood. New Edition. Crown 8vo, 3s. 6d. Cheaper Edition, 2s. 6d.
Our Poor Relations. A Philozoic Essay. With Illustrations, chiefly by Ernest Griset. Crown 8vo, cloth gilt, 3s. 6d.
The Life of General Sir Edward Bruce Hamley, K.C.B., K.C.M.G. By ALEXANDER INNES SHAND. With two Photogravure Portraits and other Illustrations. Cheaper Edition. With a Statement by Mr EDWARD HAMLEY. 2 vols. demy 8vo, 10s. 6d.

HARE. Down the Village Street: Scenes in a West Country Hamlet. By CHRISTOPHER HARE. Second Edition. Crown 8vo, 6s.

HARRADEN. In Varying Moods: Short Stories. By BEATRICE HARRADEN, Author of 'Ships that Pass in the Night.' Twelfth Edition. Crown 8vo, 3s. 6d.

HARRIS.
From Batum to Baghdad, *viâ* Tiflis, Tabriz, and Persian Kurdistan. By WALTER B. HARRIS, F.R.G.S., Author of 'The Land of an African Sultan; Travels in Morocco,' &c. With numerous Illustrations and 2 Maps. Demy 8vo, 12s.

HARRIS.
Tafilet. The Narrative of a Journey of Exploration to the
Atlas Mountains and the Oases of the North-West Sahara. With Illustrations
by Maurice Romberg from Sketches and Photographs by the Author, and Two
Maps. Demy 8vo, 12s.
A Journey through the Yemen, and some General Remarks
upon that Country. With 3 Maps and numerous Illustrations by Forestier and
Wallace from Sketches and Photographs taken by the Author. Demy 8vo, 16s.
Danovitch, and other Stories. Crown 8vo, 6s.
HAWKER. The Prose Works of Rev. R. S. HAWKER, Vicar of
Morwenstow. Including 'Footprints of Former Men in Far Cornwall.' Re-edited,
with Sketches never before published. With a Frontispiece. Crown 8vo, 3s. 6d.
HAY. The Works of the Right Rev. Dr George Hay, Bishop of
Edinburgh. Edited under the Supervision of the Right Rev. Bishop STRAIN.
With Memoir and Portrait of the Author. 5 vols. crown 8vo, bound in extra
cloth, £1, 1s. The following Volumes may be had separately—viz.:
The Devout Christian Instructed in the Law of Christ from the Written
Word. 2 vols., 8s.—The Pious Christian Instructed in the Nature and Practice
of the Principal Exercises of Piety. 1 vol., 3s.
HEATLEY.
The Horse-Owner's Safeguard. A Handy Medical Guide for
every Man who owns a Horse. By G. S. HEATLEY, M.R.C.V.S. Crown 8vo, 5s.
The Stock-Owner's Guide. A Handy Medical Treatise for
every Man who owns an Ox or a Cow. Crown 8vo, 4s. 6d.
HEDDERWICK. Lays of Middle Age; and other Poems. By
JAMES HEDDERWICK, LL.D., Author of 'Backward Glances.' Price 3s. 6d.
HEMANS.
The Poetical Works of Mrs Hemans. Copyright Editions.
Royal 8vo, 5s. The Same with Engravings, cloth, gilt edges, 7s. 6d.
Select Poems of Mrs Hemans. Fcap., cloth, gilt edges, 3s.
HERKLESS. Cardinal Beaton: Priest and Politician. By
JOHN HERKLESS, Professor of Church History, St Andrews. With a Portrait.
Post 8vo, 7s. 6d.
HEWISON. The Isle of Bute in the Olden Time. With Illus-
trations, Maps, and Plans. By JAMES KING HEWISON, M.A., F.S.A. (Scot.)
Minister of Rothesay. Vol. I., Celtic Saints and Heroes. Crown 4to, 15s. net.
Vol. II., The Royal Stewards and the Brandanes. Crown 4to, 15s. net.
HIBBEN. Inductive Logic. By JOHN GRIER HIBBEN, Ph.D.,
Assistant Professor of Logic in Princeton University, U.S.A. Crown 8vo,
3s. 6d. net.
HOME PRAYERS. By Ministers of the Church of Scotland
and Members of the Church Service Society. Second Edition. Fcap. 8vo, 3s.
HORNBY. Admiral of the Fleet Sir Geoffrey Phipps Hornby,
G.C.B. A Biography. By Mrs FRED. EGERTON. With Three Portraits. Demy
8vo, 16s.
HUTCHINSON. Hints on the Game of Golf. By HORACE G.
HUTCHINSON. Ninth Edition, Enlarged. Fcap. 8vo, cloth, 1s.
HYSLOP. The Elements of Ethics. By JAMES H. HYSLOP,
Ph.D., Instructor in Ethics, Columbia College, New York, Author of 'The
Elements of Logic.' Post 8vo, 7s. 6d. net.

IDDESLEIGH.
Lectures and Essays. By the late EARL of IDDESLEIGH,
G.C.B., D.C.L., &c. 8vo, 16s.
Life, Letters, and Diaries of Sir Stafford Northcote, First
Earl of Iddesleigh. By ANDREW LANG. With Three Portraits and a View of
Pynes. Third Edition. 2 vols. post 8vo, 31s. 6d.
POPULAR EDITION. With Portrait and View of Pynes. Post 8vo, 7s. 6d.

IGNOTUS. The Supremacy and Sufficiency of Jesus Christ, as set forth in the Epistle to the Hebrews. By IGNOTUS. Crown 8vo, 3s. 6d.

INDEX GEOGRAPHICUS : Being a List, alphabetically arranged, of the Principal Places on the Globe, with the Countries and Subdivisions of the Countries in which they are situated, and their Latitudes and Longitudes. Imperial 8vo, pp. 676, 21s.

JEAN JAMBON. Our Trip to Blunderland ; or, Grand Excursion to Blundertown and Back. By JEAN JAMBON. With Sixty Illustrations designed by CHARLES DOYLE, engraved by DALZIEL. Fourth Thousand. Cloth, gilt edges, 6s. 6d. Cheap Edition, cloth, 3s. 6d. Boards, 2s. 6d.

JEBB. A Strange Career. The Life and Adventures of JOHN GLADWYN JEBB. By his Widow. With an Introduction by H. RIDER HAGGARD, and an Electrogravure Portrait of Mr Jebb. Third Edition. Demy 8vo, 10s. 6d. CHEAP EDITION. With Illustrations by John Wallace. Crown 8vo, 3s. 6d.

Some Unconventional People. By Mrs GLADWYN JEBB, Author of 'Life and Adventures of J. G. Jebb.' With Illustrations. Crown 8vo, 3s. 6d.

JENNINGS. Mr Gladstone : A Study. By LOUIS J. JENNINGS, M.P., Author of 'Republican Government in the United States,' 'The Croker Memoirs,' &c. Popular Edition. Crown 8vo, 1s.

JERNINGHAM.

Reminiscences of an Attaché. By HUBERT E. H. JERNINGHAM. Second Edition. Crown 8vo, 5s.

Diane de Breteuille. A Love Story. Crown 8vo, 2s. 6d.

JOHNSTON.

The Chemistry of Common Life. By Professor J. F. W. JOHNSTON. New Edition, Revised. By ARTHUR HERBERT CHURCH, M.A. Oxon.; Author of 'Food: its Sources, Constituents, and Uses,' &c. With Maps and 102 Engravings. Crown 8vo, 7s. 6d.

Elements of Agricultural Chemistry. An entirely New Edition from the Edition by Sir CHARLES A. CAMERON, M.D., F.R.C.S.I., &c. Revised and brought down to date by C. M. AIKMAN, M.A., B.Sc., F.R.S.E., Professor of Chemistry, Glasgow Veterinary College. 17th Edition. Crown 8vo, 6s. 6d.

Catechism of Agricultural Chemistry. An entirely New Edition from the Edition by Sir CHARLES A. CAMERON. Revised and Enlarged by C. M. AIKMAN, M.A., &c. 95th Thousand. With numerous Illustrations. Crown 8vo, 1s.

JOHNSTON. Agricultural Holdings (Scotland) Acts, 1883 and 1889 ; and the Ground Game Act, 1880. With Notes, and Summary of Procedure, &c. By CHRISTOPHER N. JOHNSTON, M.A., Advocate. Demy 8vo, 5s.

JOKAI. Timar's Two Worlds. By MAURUS JOKAI. Authorised Translation by Mrs HEGAN KENNARD. Cheap Edition. Crown 8vo, 6s.

KEBBEL. The Old and the New : English Country Life. By T. E. KEBBEL, M.A., Author of 'The Agricultural Labourers,' 'Essays in History and Politics,' 'Life of Lord Beaconsfield.' Crown 8vo, 5s.

KERR. St Andrews in 1645-46. By D. R. KERR. Crown 8vo, 2s. 6d.

KINGLAKE.

History of the Invasion of the Crimea. By A. W. KINGLAKE. New Edition, Abridged by Lt.-Colonel Sir GEORGE S. CLARKE, K.C.M.G., R.E. With Maps and Plans. *[In preparation.*

History of the Invasion of the Crimea. By A. W. KINGLAKE. Cabinet Edition, Revised. With an Index to the Complete Work. Illustrated with Maps and Plans. Complete in 9 vols., crown 8vo, at 6s. each.

KINGLAKE.
History of the Invasion of the Crimea. Demy 8vo. Vol. VI.
Winter Troubles. With a Map, 16s. Vols. VII. and VIII. From the Morrow of
Inkerman to the Death of Lord Raglan. With an Index to the Whole Work.
With Maps and Plans. 28s.
Eothen. A New Edition, uniform with the Cabinet Edition
of the 'History of the Invasion of the Crimea.' 6s.
CHEAPER EDITION. With Portrait and Biographical Sketch of the Author.
Crown 8vo, 3s. 6d.
KIRBY. In Haunts of Wild Game: A Hunter-Naturalist's
Wanderings from Kahlamba to Libombo. By FREDERICK VAUGHAN KIRBY,
F.Z.S. (Maqaqamba). With numerous Illustrations by Charles Whymper, and a
Map. Large demy 8vo, 25s.
KLEIN. Among the Gods. Scenes of India, with Legends by
the Way. By AUGUSTA KLEIN. With 22 Full-page Illustrations. Demy 8vo, 15s.
KNEIPP. My Water-Cure. As Tested through more than
Thirty Years, and Described for the Healing of Diseases and the Preservation of
Health. By SEBASTIAN KNEIPP, Parish Priest of Wörishofen (Bavaria). With a
Portrait and other Illustrations. Authorised English Translation from the
Thirtieth German Edition, by A. de F. Cheap Edition. With an Appendix, con-
taining the Latest Developments of Pfarrer Kneipp's System, and a Preface by
E. Gerard. Crown 8vo, 3s. 6d.
KNOLLYS. The Elements of Field-Artillery. Designed for
the Use of Infantry and Cavalry Officers. By HENRY KNOLLYS, Colonel Royal
Artillery; Author of 'From Sedan to Saarbrück,' Editor of 'Incidents in the
Sepoy War,' &c. With Engravings. Crown 8vo, 7s. 6d.
LANG. Life, Letters, and Diaries of Sir Stafford Northcote,
First Earl of Iddesleigh. By ANDREW LANG. With Three Portraits and a View
of Pynes. Third Edition. 2 vols. post 8vo, 31s. 6d.
POPULAR EDITION. With Portrait and View of Pynes. Post 8vo, 7s. 6d.
LEES. A Handbook of the Sheriff and Justice of Peace Small
Debt Courts. With Notes, References, and Forms. By J. M. LEES, Advocate,
Sheriff of Stirling, Dumbarton, and Clackmannan. 8vo, 7s. 6d.
LINDSAY.
Recent Advances in Theistic Philosophy of Religion. By Rev.
JAMES LINDSAY, M.A., B.D., B.Sc., F.R.S.E., F.G.S., Minister of the Parish of
St Andrew's, Kilmarnock. Demy 8vo, 9s.
The Progressiveness of Modern Christian Thought. Crown
8vo, 6s.
Essays, Literary and Philosophical. Crown 8vo, 3s. 6d.
LOCKHART.
Doubles and Quits. By LAURENCE W. M. LOCKHART. New
Edition. Crown 8vo, 3s. 6d.
Fair to See. New Edition. Crown 8vo, 3s. 6d.
Mine is Thine. New Edition. Crown 8vo, 3s. 6d.
LOCKHART.
The Church of Scotland in the Thirteenth Century. The
Life and Times of David de Bernham of St Andrews (Bishop), A.D. 1239 to 1253.
With List of Churches dedicated by him, and Dates. By WILLIAM LOCKHART,
A.M., D.D., F.S.A. Scot., Minister of Colinton Parish. 2d Edition. 8vo, 6s.
Dies Tristes: Sermons for Seasons of Sorrow. Crown 8vo, 6s.
LORIMER.
The Institutes of Law : A Treatise of the Principles of Juris-
prudence as determined by Nature. By the late JAMES LORIMER, Professor of
Public Law and of the Law of Nature and Nations in the University of Edin-
burgh. New Edition, Revised and much Enlarged. 8vo, 18s.
The Institutes of the Law of Nations. A Treatise of the
Jural Relation of Separate Political Communities. In 2 vols. 8vo. Volume I.,
price 16s. Volume II., price 20s.

LUGARD. The Rise of our East African Empire : Early Efforts in Uganda and Nyasaland. By F. D. LUGARD, Captain Norfolk Regiment. With 130 Illustrations from Drawings and Photographs under the personal superintendence of the Author, and 14 specially prepared Maps. In 2 vols. large demy 8vo, 42s.

M'CHESNEY.
Miriam Cromwell, Royalist : A Romance of the Great Rebellion. By DORA GREENWELL M'CHESNEY. Crown 8vo, 6s.
Kathleen Clare : Her Book, 1637-41. Edited by DORA GREENWELL M'CHESNEY. With Frontispiece, and five full-page Illustrations by James A. Shearman. Crown 8vo, 6s.

M'COMBIE. Cattle and Cattle-Breeders. By WILLIAM M'COMBIE, Tillyfour. New Edition, Enlarged, with Memoir of the Author by JAMES MACDONALD, F.R.S.E., Secretary Highland and Agricultural Society of Scotland. Crown 8vo, 3s. 6d.

M'CRIE.
Works of the Rev. Thomas M'Crie, D.D. Uniform Edition. 4 vols. crown 8vo, 24s.
Life of John Knox. Crown 8vo, 6s. Another Edition, 3s. 6d.
Life of Andrew Melville. Crown 8vo, 6s.
History of the Progress and Suppression of the Reformation in Italy in the Sixteenth Century. Crown 8vo, 4s.
History of the Progress and Suppression of the Reformation in Spain in the Sixteenth Century. Crown 8vo, 3s. 6d.

M'CRIE. The Public Worship of Presbyterian Scotland. Historically treated. With copious Notes, Appendices, and Index. The Fourteenth Series of the Cunningham Lectures. By the Rev. CHARLES G. M'CRIE, D.D. Demy 8vo, 10s. 6d.

MACDONALD. A Manual of the Criminal Law (Scotland) Procedure Act, 1887. By NORMAN DORAN MACDONALD. Revised by the LORD JUSTICE-CLERK. 8vo, 10s. 6d.

MACDONALD AND SINCLAIR. History of Polled Aberdeen and Angus Cattle. Giving an Account of the Origin, Improvement, and Characteristics of the Breed. By JAMES MACDONALD and JAMES SINCLAIR. Illustrated with numerous Animal Portraits. Post 8vo, 12s. 6d.

MACDOUGALL AND DODDS. A Manual of the Local Government (Scotland) Act, 1894. With Introduction, Explanatory Notes, and Copious Index. By J. PATTEN MACDOUGALL, Legal Secretary to the Lord Advocate, and J. M. DODDS. Tenth Thousand, Revised. Crown 8vo, 2s. 6d. net.

MACINTYRE. Hindu - Koh : Wanderings and Wild Sports on and beyond the Himalayas. By Major-General DONALD MACINTYRE, V.C., late Prince of Wales' Own Goorkhas, F.R.G.S. *Dedicated to H.R.H. The Prince of Wales.* New and Cheaper Edition, Revised, with numerous Illustrations. Post 8vo, 3s. 6d.

MACKAY.
A Manual of Modern Geography ; Mathematical, Physical, and Political. By the Rev. ALEXANDER MACKAY, LL.D., F.R.G.S. 11th Thousand, Revised to the present time. Crown 8vo, pp. 688, 7s. 6d.
Elements of Modern Geography. 55th Thousand, Revised to the present time. Crown 8vo, pp. 300, 3s.
The Intermediate Geography. Intended as an Intermediate Book between the Author's 'Outlines of Geography' and 'Elements of Geography.' Eighteenth Edition, Revised. Fcap. 8vo, pp. 238, 2s.
Outlines of Modern Geography. 191st Thousand, Revised to the present time. Fcap. 8vo, pp. 128, 1s.
Elements of Physiography. New Edition. Rewritten and Enlarged. With numerous Illustrations. Crown 8vo. [*In the press.*]

MACKENZIE. Studies in Roman Law. With Comparative
Views of the Laws of France, England, and Scotland. By Lord MACKENZIE,
one of the Judges of the Court of Session in Scotland. Sixth Edition, Edited
by JOHN KIRKPATRICK, M.A., LL.B., Advocate, Professor of History in the
University of Edinburgh. 8vo, 12s.

MACPHERSON. Glimpses of Church and Social Life in the
Highlands in Olden Times. By ALEXANDER MACPHERSON, F.S.A. Scot. With
6 Photogravure Portraits and other full-page Illustrations. Small 4to, 25s.

M'PHERSON. Golf and Golfers. Past and Present. By J.
GORDON M'PHERSON, Ph.D., F.R.S.E. With an Introduction by the Right Hon.
A. J. BALFOUR, and a Portrait of the Author. Fcap. 8vo, 1s. 6d.

MACRAE. A Handbook of Deer-Stalking. By ALEXANDER
MACRAE, late Forester to Lord Henry Bentinck. With Introduction by Horatio
Ross, Esq. Fcap. 8vo, with 2 Photographs from Life. 3s. 6d.

MAIN. Three Hundred English Sonnets. Chosen and Edited
by DAVID M. MAIN. New Edition. Fcap. 8vo, 3s. 6d.

MAIR. A Digest of Laws and Decisions, Ecclesiastical and
Civil, relating to the Constitution, Practice, and Affairs of the Church of Scot-
land. With Notes and Forms of Procedure. By the Rev. WILLIAM MAIR, D.D.,
Minister of the Parish of Earlston. New Edition, Revised. Crown 8vo, 9s. net.

MARCHMONT AND THE HUMES OF POLWARTH. By
One of their Descendants. With numerous Portraits and other Illustrations.
Crown 4to, 21s. net.

MARSHMAN. History of India. From the Earliest Period to
the present time. By JOHN CLARK MARSHMAN, C.S.I. Third and Cheaper
Edition. Post 8vo, with Map, 6s.

MARTIN.
The Æneid of Virgil. Books I.-VI. Translated by Sir THEO-
DORE MARTIN, K.C.B. Post 8vo, 6s.
Goethe's Faust. Part I. Translated into English Verse.
Second Edition, crown 8vo, 6s. Ninth Edition, fcap. 8vo, 3s. 6d.
Goethe's Faust. Part II. Translated into English Verse.
Second Edition, Revised. Fcap. 8vo, 6s.
The Works of Horace. Translated into English Verse, with
Life and Notes. 2 vols. New Edition. Crown 8vo, 21s.
Poems and Ballads of Heinrich Heine. Done into English
Verse. Third Edition. Small crown 8vo, 5s.
The Song of the Bell, and other Translations from Schiller,
Goethe, Uhland, and Others. Crown 8vo, 7s. 6d.
Madonna Pia: A Tragedy; and Three Other Dramas. Crown
8vo, 7s. 6d.
Catullus. With Life and Notes. Second Edition, Revised
and Corrected. Post 8vo, 7s. 6d.
The 'Vita Nuova' of Dante. Translated, with an Introduction
and Notes. Third Edition. Small crown 8vo, 5s.
Aladdin: A Dramatic Poem. By ADAM OEHLENSCHLAEGER.
Fcap. 8vo, 5s.
Correggio: A Tragedy. By OEHLENSCHLAEGER. With Notes.
Fcap. 8vo, 3s.

MARTIN. On some of Shakespeare's Female Characters. By
HELENA FAUCIT, Lady MARTIN. Dedicated by permission to Her Most Gracious
Majesty the Queen. Fifth Edition. With a Portrait by Lehmann. Demy
8vo, 7s. 6d.

MARWICK. Observations on the Law and Practice in regard
to Municipal Elections and the Conduct of the Business of Town Councils and
Commissioners of Police in Scotland. By Sir JAMES D. MARWICK, LL.D.,
Town-Clerk of Glasgow. Royal 8vo, 30s.

MATHESON.
Can the Old Faith Live with the New ? or, The Problem of Evolution and Revelation. By the Rev. GEORGE MATHESON, D.D. Third Edition. Crown 8vo, 7s. 6d.
The Psalmist and the Scientist ; or, Modern Value of the Religious Sentiment. Third Edition. Crown 8vo, 5s.
Spiritual Development of St Paul. Third Edition. Cr. 8vo, 5s.
The Distinctive Messages of the Old Religions. Second Edition. Crown 8vo, 5s.
Sacred Songs. New and Cheaper Edition. Crown 8vo, 2s. 6d.

MAURICE. The Balance of Military Power in Europe. An Examination of the War Resources of Great Britain and the Continental States. By Colonel MAURICE, R.A., Professor of Military Art and History at the Royal Staff College. Crown 8vo, with a Map, 6s.

MAXWELL.
A Duke of Britain. A Romance of the Fourth Century. By Sir HERBERT MAXWELL, Bart., M.P., F.S.A., &c., Author of 'Passages in the Life of Sir Lucian Elphin.' Fourth Edition. Crown 8vo, 6s.
Life and Times of the Rt. Hon. William Henry Smith, M.P. With Portraits and numerous Illustrations by Herbert Railton, G. L. Seymour, and Others. 2 vols. demy 8vo, 25s.
POPULAR EDITION. With a Portrait and other Illustrations. Crown 8vo, 3s. 6d.
Scottish Land-Names : Their Origin and Meaning. Being the Rhind Lectures in Archæology for 1893. Post 8vo, 6s.
Meridiana : Noontide Essays. Post 8vo, 7s. 6d.
Post Meridiana : Afternoon Essays. Post 8vo, 6s.
Dumfries and Galloway. Being one of the Volumes of the County Histories of Scotland. With Two Maps. Demy 8vo, 7s. 6d. *net.*

MELDRUM.
The Story of Margrédel : Being a Fireside History of a Fifeshire Family. By D. STORRAR MELDRUM. Cheap Edition. Crown 8vo, 3s. 6d.
Grey Mantle and Gold Fringe. Crown 8vo, 6s.

MERZ. A History of European Thought in the Nineteenth Century. By JOHN THEODORE MERZ. Vol. I., post 8vo. [*Immediately.*

MICHEL. A Critical Inquiry into the Scottish Language. With the view of Illustrating the Rise and Progress of Civilisation in Scotland. By FRANCISQUE-MICHEL, F.S.A. Lond. and Scot., Correspondant de l'Institut de France, &c. 4to, printed on hand-made paper, and bound in roxburghe, 66s.

MICHIE.
The Larch : Being a Practical Treatise on its Culture and General Management. By CHRISTOPHER Y. MICHIE, Forester, Cullen House. Crown 8vo, with Illustrations. New and Cheaper Edition, Enlarged, 5s.
The Practice of Forestry. Crown 8vo, with Illustrations. 6s.

MIDDLETON. The Story of Alastair Bhan Comyn ; or, The Tragedy of Dunphail. A Tale of Tradition and Romance. By the Lady MIDDLETON. Square 8vo, 10s. Cheaper Edition, 5s.

MILLER. The Story of Mr H——, the Herbalist. By HUGH MILLER, F.R.S.E., late H.M. Geological Survey, Author of 'Landscape Geology.' With a Photogravure Frontispiece. Crown 8vo, 2s. 6d.

MINTO.
A Manual of English Prose Literature, Biographical and Critical : designed mainly to show Characteristics of Style. By W. MINTO, M.A., Hon. LL.D. of St Andrews ; Professor of Logic in the University of Aberdeen. Third Edition, Revised. Crown 8vo, 7s. 6d.
Characteristics of English Poets, from Chaucer to Shirley. New Edition, Revised. Crown 8vo, 7s. 6d.
Plain Principles of Prose Composition. Crown 8vo, 1s. 6d.

MINTO.
The Literature of the Georgian Era. Edited, with a Biographical Introduction, by Professor KNIGHT, St Andrews. Post 8vo, 6s.

MOIR. Life of Mansie Wauch, Tailor in Dalkeith. By D. M.
MOIR. With CRUIKSHANK'S Illustrations. Cheaper Edition. Crown 8vo, 2s. 6d.
Another Edition, without Illustrations, fcap. 8vo, 1s. 6d.

MOLE. For the Sake of a Slandered Woman. By MARION
MOLE. Fcap. 8vo, 2s. 6d. net.

MOMERIE.
Defects of Modern Christianity, and other Sermons. By
ALFRED WILLIAMS MOMERIE, M.A., D.Sc., LL.D. Fifth Edition. Crown
8vo, 5s.
The Basis of Religion. Being an Examination of Natural
Religion. Third Edition. Crown 8vo, 2s. 6d.
The Origin of Evil, and other Sermons. Eighth Edition,
Enlarged. Crown 8vo, 5s.
Personality. The Beginning and End of Metaphysics, and
a Necessary Assumption in all Positive Philosophy. Fifth Edition, Revised.
Crown 8vo, 3s.
Agnosticism. Fourth Edition, Revised. Crown 8vo, 5s.
Preaching and Hearing ; and other Sermons. Fourth Edition,
Enlarged. Crown 8vo, 5s.
Belief in God. Third Edition. Crown 8vo, 3s.
Inspiration ; and other Sermons. Second Edition, Enlarged.
Crown 8vo, 5s.
Church and Creed. Third Edition. Crown 8vo, 4s. 6d.
The Future of Religion, and other Essays. Second Edition.
Crown 8vo, 3s. 6d.

MONCREIFF.
The Provost-Marshal. A Romance of the Middle Shires. By
the Hon. FREDERICK MONCREIFF. Crown 8vo, 6s.
The X Jewel. A Romance of the Days of James VI. Crown
8vo, 6s.

MONTAGUE. Military Topography. Illustrated by Practical
Examples of a Practical Subject. By Major-General W. E. MONTAGUE, C.B.,
P.S.C., late Garrison Instructor Intelligence Department, Author of 'Campaign-
ing in South Africa.' With Forty-one Diagrams. Crown 8vo, 5s.

MONTALEMBERT. Memoir of Count de Montalembert. A
Chapter of Recent French History. By Mrs OLIPHANT, Author of the 'Life of
Edward Irving,' &c. 2 vols. crown 8vo, £1, 4s.

MORISON.
Doorside Ditties. By JEANIE MORISON. With a Frontis-
piece. Crown 8vo, 3s. 6d.
Æolus. A Romance in Lyrics. Crown 8vo, 3s.
There as Here. Crown 8vo, 3s.
 ₌ *A limited impression on hand-made paper, bound in vellum, 7s. 6d.*
Selections from Poems. Crown 8vo, 4s. 6d.
Sordello. An Outline Analysis of Mr Browning's Poem
Crown 8vo, 3s.
Of "Fifine at the Fair," "Christmas Eve and Easter Day,'
and other of Mr Browning's Poems. Crown 8vo, 3s.
The Purpose of the Ages. Crown 8vo, 9s.
Gordon : An Our-day Idyll. Crown 8vo, 3s.
Saint Isadora, and other Poems. Crown 8vo, 1s. 6d.
Snatches of Song. Paper, 1s. 6d. ; cloth, 3s.
Pontius Pilate. Paper, 1s. 6d. ; cloth, 3s.

MORISON.
Mill o' Forres. Crown 8vo, 1s.
Ane Booke of Ballades. Fcap. 4to, 1s.

MOZLEY. Essays from 'Blackwood.' By the late ANNE
MOZLEY, Author of 'Essays on Social Subjects'; Editor of 'The Letters and
Correspondence of Cardinal Newman,' 'Letters of the Rev. J. B. Mozley,' &c.
With a Memoir by her Sister, FANNY MOZLEY. Post 8vo, 7s. 6d.

MUNRO. The Lost Pibroch, and other Sheiling Stories. By
NEIL MUNRO. Crown 8vo, 6s.

MUNRO. Rambles and Studies in Bosnia - Herzegovina and
Dalmatia. With an Account of the Proceedings of the Congress of Archæolo-
gists and Anthropologists held at Sarajevo in 1894. By ROBERT MUNRO, M.A.,
M.D., F.R.S.E., Author of 'The Lake-Dwellings of Europe,' &c. With numerous
Illustrations. Demy 8vo, 12s. 6d. net.

MUNRO. On Valuation of Property. By WILLIAM MUNRO,
M.A., Her Majesty's Assessor of Railways and Canals for Scotland. Second
Edition, Revised and Enlarged. 8vo, 3s. 6d.

MURDOCH. Manual of the Law of Insolvency and Bankruptcy:
Comprehending a Summary of the Law of Insolvency, Notour Bankruptcy,
Composition - Contracts, Trust - Deeds, Cessios, and Sequestrations; and the
Winding-up of Joint-Stock Companies in Scotland; with Annotations on the
various Insolvency and Bankruptcy Statutes; and with Forms of Procedure
applicable to these Subjects. By JAMES MURDOCH, Member of the Faculty of
Procurators in Glasgow. Fifth Edition, Revised and Enlarged. 8vo, 12s. net.

**MY TRIVIAL LIFE AND MISFORTUNE : A Gossip with
no Plot in Particular. By A PLAIN WOMAN. Cheap Edition. Crown 8vo, 3s. 6d.
By the SAME AUTHOR.**

POOR NELLIE. Cheap Edition. Crown 8vo, 3s. 6d.

MY WEATHER - WISE COMPANION. Presented by B. T.
Fcap. 8vo, 1s. net.

NAPIER. The Construction of the Wonderful Canon of Loga-
rithms. By JOHN NAPIER of Merchiston. Translated, with Notes, and a
Catalogue of Napier's Works, by WILLIAM RAE MACDONALD. Small 4to, 15s.
A few large-paper copies on Whatman paper, 30s.

NEAVES. Songs and Verses, Social and Scientific. By An Old
Contributor to 'Maga.' By the Hon. Lord NEAVES. Fifth Edition. Fcap.
8vo, 4s.

NICHOLSON.
A Manual of Zoology, for the Use of Students. With a
General Introduction on the Principles of Zoology. By HENRY ALLEYNE
NICHOLSON, M.D., D.Sc., F.L.S., F.G.S., Regius Professor of Natural History in
the University of Aberdeen. Seventh Edition, Rewritten and Enlarged. Post
8vo, pp. 956, with 555 Engravings on Wood, 18s.

Text-Book of Zoology, for Junior Students. Fifth Edition,
Rewritten and Enlarged. Crown 8vo, with 358 Engravings on Wood, 10s. 6d.

Introductory Text-Book of Zoology, for the Use of Junior
Classes. Sixth Edition, Revised and Enlarged, with 166 Engravings, 3s.

Outlines of Natural History, for Beginners : being Descriptions of a Progressive Series of Zoological Types. Third Edition, with
Engravings, 1s. 6d.

A Manual of Palæontology, for the Use of Students. With a
General Introduction on the Principles of Palæontology. By Professor H.
ALLEYNE NICHOLSON and RICHARD LYDEKKER, B.A. Third Edition, entirely
Rewritten and greatly Enlarged. 2 vols. 8vo, £3, 3s.

The Ancient Life-History of the Earth. An Outline of the
Principles and Leading Facts of Palæontological Science. Crown 8vo, with 276
Engravings, 10s. 6d.

NICHOLSON.

On the "Tabulate Corals" of the Palæozoic Period, with Critical Descriptions of Illustrative Species. Illustrated with 15 Lithographed Plates and numerous Engravings. Super-royal 8vo, 21s.

Synopsis of the Classification of the Animal Kingdom. 8vo, with 106 Illustrations, 6s.

On the Structure and Affinities of the Genus Monticulipora and its Sub-Genera, with Critical Descriptions of Illustrative Species. Illustrated with numerous Engravings on Wood and Lithographed Plates. Super-royal 8vo, 18s.

NICHOLSON.

Thoth. A Romance. By JOSEPH SHIELD NICHOLSON, M.A., D.Sc., Professor of Commercial and Political Economy and Mercantile Law in the University of Edinburgh. Third Edition. Crown 8vo, 4s. 6d.

A Dreamer of Dreams. A Modern Romance. Second Edition. Crown 8vo, 6s.

NICOLSON AND MURE. A Handbook to the Local Government (Scotland) Act, 1889. With Introduction, Explanatory Notes, and Index. By J. BADENACH NICOLSON, Advocate, Counsel to the Scotch Education Department, and W. J. MURE, Advocate, Legal Secretary to the Lord Advocate for Scotland. Ninth Reprint. 8vo, 5s.

OLIPHANT.

Masollam : A Problem of the Period. A Novel. By LAURENCE OLIPHANT. 3 vols. post 8vo, 25s. 6d.

Scientific Religion ; or, Higher Possibilities of Life and Practice through the Operation of Natural Forces. Second Edition. 8vo, 16s.

Altiora Peto. Cheap Edition. Crown 8vo, boards, 2s. 6d. ; cloth, 3s. 6d. Illustrated Edition. Crown 8vo, cloth, 6s.

Piccadilly. With Illustrations by Richard Doyle. New Edition, 3s. 6d. Cheap Edition, boards, 2s. 6d.

Traits and Travesties ; Social and Political. Post 8vo, 10s. 6d.

Episodes in a Life of Adventure ; or, Moss from a Rolling Stone. Cheaper Edition. Post 8vo, 3s. 6d.

Haifa : Life in Modern Palestine. Second Edition. 8vo, 7s. 6d.

The Land of Gilead. With Excursions in the Lebanon. With Illustrations and Maps. Demy 8vo, 21s.

Memoir of the Life of Laurence Oliphant, and of Alice Oliphant, his Wife. By Mrs M. O. W. OLIPHANT. Seventh Edition. 2 vols. post 8vo, with Portraits. 21s.

POPULAR EDITION. With a New Preface. Post 8vo, with Portraits. 7s. 6d.

OLIPHANT.

Who was Lost and is Found. By Mrs OLIPHANT. Second Edition. Crown 8vo, 6s.

Miss Marjoribanks. New Edition. Crown 8vo, 3s. 6d.

The Perpetual Curate, and The Rector. New Edition. Crown 8vo, 3s. 6d.

Salem Chapel, and The Doctor's Family. New Edition. Crown 8vo, 3s. 6d.

Katie Stewart, and other Stories. New Edition. Crown 8vo, cloth, 3s. 6d.

Katie Stewart. Illustrated boards, 2s. 6d.

Valentine and his Brother. New Edition. Crown 8vo, 3s. 6d.

Sons and Daughters. Crown 8vo, 3s. 6d.

Two Stories of the Seen and the Unseen. The Open Door —Old Lady Mary. Paper covers, 1s.

OLIPHANT. Notes of a Pilgrimage to Jerusalem and the Holy
Land. By F. R. OLIPHANT. Crown 8vo, 3s. 6d.

OSWALD. By Fell and Fjord; or, Scenes and Studies in Ice-
land. By E. J. OSWALD. Post 8vo, with Illustrations. 7s. 6d.

PAGE.

Introductory Text-Book of Geology. By DAVID PAGE, LL.D.,
Professor of Geology in the Durham University of Physical Science, Newcastle.
With Engravings and Glossarial Index. New Edition. Revised by Professor
LAPWORTH of Mason Science College, Birmingham. [*In preparation.*

Advanced Text-Book of Geology, Descriptive and Industrial.
With Engravings, and Glossary of Scientific Terms. New Edition. Revised by
Professor LAPWORTH. [*In preparation.*

Introductory Text-Book of Physical Geography. With Sketch-
Maps and Illustrations. Edited by Professor LAPWORTH, LL.D., F.G.S., &c.,
Mason Science College, Birmingham. Thirteenth Edition, Revised and Enlarged.
2s. 6d.

Advanced Text-Book of Physical Geography. Third Edition.
Revised and Enlarged by Professor LAPWORTH. With Engravings. 5s.

PATON.

Spindrift. By Sir J. NOEL PATON. Fcap., cloth, 5s.

Poems by a Painter. Fcap., cloth, 5s.

PATON. Body and Soul. A Romance in Transcendental Path-
ology. By FREDERICK NOEL PATON. Third Edition. Crown 8vo, 1s.

PATRICK. The Apology of Origen in Reply to Celsus. A
Chapter in the History of Apologetics. By the Rev. J. PATRICK, D.D. Post 8vo,
7s. 6d.

PAUL. History of the Royal Company of Archers, the Queen's
Body-Guard for Scotland. By JAMES BALFOUR PAUL, Advocate of the Scottish
Bar. Crown 4to, with Portraits and other Illustrations. £2, 2s.

PEILE. Lawn Tennis as a Game of Skill. By Lieut.-Col. S. C.
F. PEILE, B.S.C. Revised Edition, with new Scoring Rules. Fcap. 8vo, cloth, 1s.

PETTIGREW. The Handy Book of Bees, and their Profitable
Management. By A. PETTIGREW. Fifth Edition, Enlarged, with Engravings.
Crown 8vo, 3s. 6d.

PFLEIDERER. Philosophy and Development of Religion.
Being the Edinburgh Gifford Lectures for 1894. By OTTO PFLEIDERER, D.D.
Professor of Theology at Berlin University. In 2 vols. post 8vo, 15s. net.

PHILOSOPHICAL CLASSICS FOR ENGLISH READERS.
Edited by WILLIAM KNIGHT, LL.D., Professor of Moral Philosophy, University
of St Andrews. In crown 8vo volumes, with Portraits, price 3s. 6d.
[*For List of Volumes, see page 2.*

POLLARD. A Study in Municipal Government: The Corpora-
tion of Berlin. By JAMES POLLARD, C.A., Chairman of the Edinburgh Public
Health Committee, and Secretary of the Edinburgh Chamber of Commerce.
Second Edition, Revised. Crown 8vo, 3s. 6d.

POLLOK. The Course of Time: A Poem. By ROBERT POLLOK,
A.M. Cottage Edition, 32mo, 8d. The Same, cloth, gilt edges, 1s. 6d. Another
Edition, with Illustrations by Birket Foster and others, fcap., cloth, 3s. 6d., or
with edges gilt, 4s.

PORT ROYAL LOGIC. Translated from the French; with
Introduction, Notes, and Appendix. By THOMAS SPENCER BAYNES, LL.D., Professor in the University of St Andrews. Tenth Edition, 12mo, 4s.

POTTS AND DARNELL.

Aditus Faciliores: An Easy Latin Construing Book, with
Complete Vocabulary By A. W. POTTS, M.A., LL.D., and the Rev. C. DARNELL,
M.A., Head-Master of Cargilfield Preparatory School Edinburgh. Tenth Edition,
fcap. 8vo, 3s. 6d.

POTTS AND DARNELL.
Aditus Faciliores Graeci. An Easy Greek Construing Book,
with Complete Vocabulary. Fifth Edition, Revised. Fcap. 8vo, 3s.

POTTS. School Sermons. By the late ALEXANDER WM. POTTS,
LL.D., First Head-Master of Fettes College. With a Memoir and Portrait.
Crown 8vo, 7s. 6d.

PRINGLE. The Live Stock of the Farm. By ROBERT O.
PRINGLE. Third Edition. Revised and Edited by JAMES MACDONALD. Crown
8vo, 7s. 6d.

PRYDE. Pleasant Memories of a Busy Life. By DAVID PRYDE,
M.A., LL.D., Author of 'Highways of Literature,' 'Great Men in European History,' 'Biographical Outlines of English Literature,' &c. With a Mezzotint Portrait. Post 8vo, 6s.

PUBLIC GENERAL STATUTES AFFECTING SCOTLAND
from 1707 to 1847, with Chronological Table and Index. 3 vols. large 8vo, £3, 3s.

PUBLIC GENERAL STATUTES AFFECTING SCOTLAND,
COLLECTION OF. Published Annually, with General Index.

RAE. The Syrian Church in India. By GEORGE MILNE RAE,
M.A., D.D., Fellow of the University of Madras; late Professor in the Madras
Christian College. With 6 full-page Illustrations. Post 8vo, 10s. 6d.

RAMSAY. Scotland and Scotsmen in the Eighteenth Century.
Edited from the MSS. of JOHN RAMSAY, Esq. of Ochtertyre, by ALEXANDER
ALLARDYCE, Author of 'Memoir of Admiral Lord Keith, K.B.,' &c. 2 vols.
8vo, 31s. 6d.

RANKIN.
A Handbook of the Church of Scotland. By JAMES RANKIN,
D.D., Minister of Muthill; Author of 'Character Studies in the Old Testament,'
&c. An entirely New and much Enlarged Edition. Crown 8vo, with 2 Maps,
7s. 6d.
The First Saints. Post 8vo, 7s. 6d.
The Creed in Scotland. An Exposition of the Apostles
Creed. With Extracts from Archbishop Hamilton's Catechism of 1552, John
Calvin's Catechism of 1556, and a Catena of Ancient Latin and other Hymns.
Post 8vo, 7s. 6d.
The Worthy Communicant. A Guide to the Devout Obser-
vance of the Lord's Supper. Limp cloth, 1s. 3d.
The Young Churchman. Lessons on the Creed, the Com-
mandments, the Means of Grace, and the Church. Limp cloth, 1s. 3d.
First Communion Lessons. 25th Edition. Paper Cover, 2d.

RANKINE. A Hero of the Dark Continent. Memoir of Rev.
Wm. Affleck Scott, M.A., M.B., C.M., Church of Scotland Missionary at Blantyre,
British Central Africa. By W. HENRY RANKINE, B.D., Minister at St Boswells.
With a Portrait and other Illustrations. Crown 8vo, 5s.

RECORDS OF THE TERCENTENARY FESTIVAL OF THE
UNIVERSITY OF EDINBURGH. Celebrated in April 1884. Published under
the Sanction of the Senatus Academicus. Large 4to, £2, 12s. 6d.

ROBERTSON. The Early Religion of Israel. As set forth by
Biblical Writers and Modern Critical Historians. Being the Baird Lecture for
1888-89. By JAMES ROBERTSON, D.D., Professor of Oriental Languages in the
University of Glasgow. Fourth Edition. Crown 8vo, 10s. 6d.

ROBERTSON.
Orellana, and other Poems. By J. LOGIE ROBERTSON,
M.A. Fcap. 8vo. Printed on hand-made paper. 6s.
A History of English Literature. For Secondary Schools.
With an Introduction by Professor MASSON, Edinburgh University. Cr. 8vo, 3s.

ROBERTSON.
English Verse for Junior Classes. In Two Parts. Part I.—
Chaucer to Coleridge. Part II.—Nineteenth Century Poets. Crown 8vo, each
1s. 6d. net.

ROBERTSON. Our Holiday among the Hills. By JAMES and
JANET LOGIE ROBERTSON. Fcap. 8vo, 3s. 6d.

ROBERTSON. Essays and Sermons. By the late W. ROBERT-
SON, B.D., Minister of the Parish of Sprouston. With a Memoir and Portrait.
Crown 8vo, 5s. 6d.

RODGER. Aberdeen Doctors at Home and Abroad. The Story
of a Medical School. By ELLA HILL BURTON RODGER. Demy 8vo, 10s. 6d.

ROSCOE. Rambles with a Fishing-Rod. By E. S. ROSCOE.
Crown 8vo, 4s. 6d.

ROSS AND SOMERVILLE. Beggars on Horseback : A Riding
Tour in North Wales. By MARTIN ROSS and E. Œ. SOMERVILLE. With Illustrations by E. Œ. SOMERVILLE. Crown 8vo, 3s. 6d.

RUTLAND.
Notes of an Irish Tour in 1846. By the DUKE OF RUTLAND,
G.C.B. (Lord JOHN MANNERS). New Edition. Crown 8vo, 2s. 6d.
Correspondence between the Right Honble. William Pitt
and Charles Duke of Rutland, Lord - Lieutenant of Ireland, 1781-1787. With
Introductory Note by JOHN DUKE OF RUTLAND. 8vo, 7s. 6d.

RUTLAND.
Gems of German Poetry. Translated by the DUCHESS OF
RUTLAND (Lady JOHN MANNERS).   [*New Edition in preparation.*
Impressions of Bad-Homburg. Comprising a Short Account
of the Women's Associations of Germany under the Red Cross. Crown 8vo, 1s. 6d.
Some Personal Recollections of the Later Years of the Earl
of Beaconsfield, K.G. Sixth Edition. 6d.
Employment of Women in the Public Service. 6d.
Some of the Advantages of Easily Accessible Reading and
Recreation Rooms and Free Libraries. With Remarks on Starting and Main-
taining them. Second Edition. Crown 8vo, 1s.
A Sequel to Rich Men's Dwellings, and other Occasional
Papers. Crown 8vo, 2s. 6d.
Encouraging Experiences of Reading and Recreation Rooms,
Aims of Guilds, Nottingham Social Guide, Existing Institutions, &c., &c.
Crown 8vo, 1s.

SAINTSBURY. The Flourishing of Romance and the Rise of
Allegory (12th and 13th Centuries). By GEORGE SAINTSBURY, M.A., Professor of
Rhetoric and English Literature in Edinburgh University. Being the first vol-
ume issued of "PERIODS OF EUROPEAN LITERATURE." Edited by Professor
SAINTSBURY. Crown 8vo, 3s. 6d.

SALMON. Songs of a Heart's Surrender, and other Verse.
By ARTHUR L. SALMON. Fcap. 8vo, 2s.

SCHEFFEL. The Trumpeter. A Romance of the Rhine. By
JOSEPH VICTOR VON SCHEFFEL. Translated from the Two Hundredth German
Edition by JESSIE BECK and LOUISA LORIMER. With an Introduction by Sir
THEODORE MARTIN, K.C.B. Long 8vo, 3s. 6d.

SCHILLER. Wallenstein. A Dramatic Poem. By FRIEDRICH
VON SCHILLER. Translated by C. G. N. LOCKHART. Fcap. 8vo, 7s. 6d.

SCOTT. Tom Cringle's Log. By MICHAEL SCOTT. New Edition.
With 19 Full-page Illustrations. Crown 8vo, 3s. 6d.

SCOUGAL. Prisons and their Inmates ; or, Scenes from a
Silent World. By FRANCIS SCOUGAL. Crown 8vo, boards, 2s.

SELKIRK. Poems. By J. B. SELKIRK, Author of 'Ethics and
Æsthetics of Modern Poetry,' 'Bible Truths with Shakespearian Parallels,' &c.
Crown 8vo, printed on antique paper, 6s.

SELLAR'S Manual of the Acts relating to Education in Scotland. By J. EDWARD GRAHAM, B.A. Oxon., Advocate. Ninth Edition. Demy
8vo, 12s. 6d.

SETH.
Scottish Philosophy. A Comparison of the Scottish and
German Answers to Hume. Balfour Philosophical Lectures, University of
Edinburgh. By ANDREW SETH, LL.D., Professor of Logic and Metaphysics in
Edinburgh University. Second Edition. Crown 8vo, 5s.
Hegelianism and Personality. Balfour Philosophical Lectures.
Second Series. Second Edition. Crown 8vo, 5s.

SETH. A Study of Ethical Principles. By JAMES SETH, M.A.,
Professor of Philosophy in Cornell University, U.S.A. Second Edition, Revised.
Post 8vo, 10s. 6d. net.

SHADWELL. The Life of Colin Campbell, Lord Clyde. Illustrated by Extracts from his Diary and Correspondence. By Lieutenant-General
SHADWELL, C.B. With Portrait, Maps, and Plans. 2 vols. 8vo, 36s.

SHAND.
The Life of General Sir Edward Bruce Hamley, K.C.B.,
K.C.M.G. By ALEX. INNES SHAND, Author of 'Kilcarra,' 'Against Time,' &c.
With two Photogravure Portraits and other Illustrations. Cheaper Edition, with
a Statement by Mr Edward Hamley. 2 vols. demy 8vo, 10s. 6d.
Half a Century; or, Changes in Men and Manners. Second
Edition. 8vo, 12s. 6d.
Letters from the West of Ireland. Reprinted from the
'Times.' Crown 8vo, 5s.

SHARPE. Letters from and to Charles Kirkpatrick Sharpe.
Edited by ALEXANDER ALLARDYCE, Author of 'Memoir of Admiral Lord Keith,
K.B.,' &c. With a Memoir by the Rev. W. K. R. BEDFORD. In 2 vols. 8vo.
Illustrated with Etchings and other Engravings. £2, 12s. 6d.

SIM. Margaret Sim's Cookery. With an Introduction by L. B.
WALFORD, Author of 'Mr Smith: A Part of his Life,' &c. Crown 8vo, 5s.

SIMPSON. The Wild Rabbit in a New Aspect; or, Rabbit-
Warrens that Pay. A book for Landowners, Sportsmen, Land Agents, Farmers,
Gamekeepers, and Allotment Holders. A Record of Recent Experiments con-
ducted on the Estate of the Right Hon. the Earl of Wharncliffe at Wortley Hall.
By J. SIMPSON. Second Edition, Enlarged. Small crown 8vo, 5s.

SKELTON.
The Table-Talk of Shirley. By JOHN SKELTON, Advocate,
C.B., LL.D., Author of 'The Essays of Shirley.' With a Frontispiece. Sixth
Edition, Revised and Enlarged. Post 8vo, 7s. 6d.
The Table-Talk of Shirley. Second Series. Summers and
Winters at Balmawhapple. With Illustrations. Two Volumes. Post 8vo, 10s.
net.
Maitland of Lethington; and the Scotland of Mary Stuart.
A History. Limited Edition, with Portraits. Demy 8vo, 2 vols., 28s. net.
The Handbook of Public Health. A Complete Edition of the
Public Health and other Sanitary Acts relating to Scotland. Annotated, and
with the Rules, Instructions, and Decisions of the Board of Supervision brought
up to date with relative forms. Second Edition. With Introduction, containing
the Administration of the Public Health Act in Counties. 8vo, 8s. 6d.
The Local Government (Scotland) Act in Relation to Public
Health. A Handy Guide for County and District Councillors, Medical Officers,
Sanitary Inspectors, and Members of Parochial Boards. Second Edition. With
a new Preface on appointment of Sanitary Officers. Crown 8vo, 2s.

SKRINE.   Columba: A Drama.   By JOHN HUNTLEY SKRINE,
Warden of Glenalmond ; Author of 'A Memory of Edward Thring.' Fcap. 4to, 6s.

SMITH.

Thorndale ; or, The Conflict of Opinions.   By WILLIAM SMITH,
Author of 'A Discourse on Ethics,' &c.   New Edition.   Crown 8vo, 10s. 6d.

Gravenhurst ; or, Thoughts on Good and Evil.   Second Edition.   With Memoir and Portrait of the Author.   Crown 8vo, 8s.

The Story of William and Lucy Smith.   Edited by GEORGE
MERRIAM.   Large post 8vo, 12s. 6d.

SMITH.   Memoir of the Families of M'Combie and Thoms,
originally M'Intosh and M'Thomas.   Compiled from History and Tradition.   By
WILLIAM M'COMBIE SMITH.   With Illustrations.   8vo, 7s. 6d.

SMITH.   Greek Testament Lessons for Colleges, Schools, and
Private Students, consisting chiefly of the Sermon on the Mount and the Parables
of our Lord.   With Notes and Essays.   By the Rev. J. HUNTER SMITH, M.A.,
King Edward's School, Birmingham.   Crown 8vo, 6s.

SMITH.   The Secretary for Scotland.   Being a Statement of the
Powers and Duties of the new Scottish Office.   With a Short Historical Intro-
duction, and numerous references to important Administrative Documents.   By
W. C. SMITH, LL.B., Advocate.   8vo, 6s.

"SON OF THE MARSHES, A."

From Spring to Fall ; or, When Life Stirs.   By "A SON OF
THE MARSHES."   Cheap Uniform Edition.   Crown 8vo, 3s. 6d.

Within an Hour of London Town : Among Wild Birds and
their Haunts.   Edited by J. A. OWEN.   Cheap Uniform Edition.   Crown 8vo,
3s. 6d.

With the Woodlanders and by the Tide.   Cheap Uniform
Edition.   Crown 8vo, 3s. 6d.

On Surrey Hills.   Cheap Uniform Edition.   Crown 8vo, 3s. 6d.

Annals of a Fishing Village.   Cheap Uniform Edition.   Crown
8vo, 3s. 6d.

SORLEY.   The Ethics of Naturalism.   Being the Shaw Fellowship Lectures, 1884.   By W. R. SORLEY, M.A., Fellow of Trinity College, Cambridge, Professor of Moral Philosophy in the University of Aberdeen.   Crown
8vo, 6s.

SPEEDY.   Sport in the Highlands and Lowlands of Scotland
with Rod and Gun.   By TOM SPEEDY.   Second Edition, Revised and Enlarged.
With Illustrations by Lieut.-General Hope Crealocke, C.B., C.M.G., and others.
8vo, 15s.

SPROTT.   The Worship and Offices of the Church of Scotland.
By GEORGE W. SPROTT, D.D., Minister of North Berwick.   Crown 8vo, 6s.

STATISTICAL ACCOUNT OF SCOTLAND.   Complete, with
Index.   15 vols. 8vo, £16, 16s.

STEPHENS.

The Book of the Farm ; detailing the Labours of the Farmer,
Farm-Steward, Ploughman, Shepherd, Hedger, Farm-Labourer, Field-Worker,
and Cattle-man.   Illustrated with numerous Portraits of Animals and Engravings
of Implements, and Plans of Farm Buildings.   Fourth Edition.   Revised, and
in great part Rewritten by JAMES MACDONALD, F.R.S.E., Secretary Highland
and Agricultural Society of Scotland.   Complete in Six Divisional Volumes,
bound in cloth, each 10s. 6d., or handsomely bound, in 3 volumes, with leather
back and gilt top, £3, 3s.

Catechism of Practical Agriculture.   22d Thousand.   Revised
by JAMES MACDONALD, F.R.S.E.   With numerous Illustrations.   Crown 8vo, 1s.

The Book of Farm Implements and Machines.   By J. SLIGHT
and R. SCOTT BURN, Engineers.   Edited by HENRY STEPHENS.   Large 8vo, £2, 2s.

STEVENSON. British Fungi. (Hymenomycetes.) By Rev.
JOHN STEVENSON, Author of 'Mycologia Scotica,' Hon. Sec. Cryptogamic Society
of Scotland. Vols. I. and II., post 8vo, with Illustrations, price 12s. 6d. net each.

STEWART. Advice to Purchasers of Horses. By JOHN
STEWART, V.S. New Edition. 2s. 6d.

STEWART. Boethius: An Essay. By HUGH FRASER STEWART,
M.A., Trinity College, Cambridge. Crown 8vo, 7s. 6d.

STODDART. Angling Songs. By THOMAS TOD STODDART.
New Edition, with a Memoir by ANNA M. STODDART. Crown 8vo, 7s. 6d.

STODDART.

John Stuart Blackie: A Biography. By ANNA M. STODDART.
With 3 Plates. Third Edition. 2 vols. demy 8vo, 21s.
POPULAR EDITION, with Portrait. Crown 8vo, 6s.

Sir Philip Sidney: Servant of God. Illustrated by MARGARET
L. HUGGINS. With a New Portrait of Sir Philip Sidney. Small 4to, with a
specially designed Cover. 5s.

STORMONTH.

Dictionary of the English Language, Pronouncing, Etymological, and Explanatory. By the Rev. JAMES STORMONTH. Revised by the
Rev. P. H. PHELP. Library Edition. New and Cheaper Edition, with Supplement. Imperial 8vo, handsomely bound in half morocco, 18s. net.

Etymological and Pronouncing Dictionary of the English
Language. Including a very Copious Selection of Scientific Terms. For use in
Schools and Colleges, and as a Book of General Reference. The Pronunciation
carefully revised by the Rev. P. H. PHELP, M.A. Cantab. Thirteenth Edition,
with Supplement. Crown 8vo, pp. 800. 7s. 6d.

The School Etymological Dictionary and Word-Book. New
Edition, Revised. [*In preparation.*

STORY.

Nero; A Historical Play. By W. W. STORY, Author of
'Roba di Roma.' Fcap. 8vo, 6s.

Vallombrosa. Post 8vo, 5s.

Poems. 2 vols., 7s. 6d.

Fiammetta. A Summer Idyl. Crown 8vo, 7s. 6d.

Conversations in a Studio. 2 vols. crown 8vo, 12s. 6d.

Excursions in Art and Letters. Crown 8vo, 7s. 6d.

A Poet's Portfolio: Later Readings. 18mo, 3s. 6d.

STRACHEY. Talk at a Country House. Fact and Fiction.
By Sir EDWARD STRACHEY, Bart. With a Portrait of the Author. Crown 8vo,
4s. 6d. net.

STURGIS. Little Comedies, Old and New. By JULIAN STURGIS.
Crown 8vo, 7s. 6d.

SUTHERLAND. Handbook of Hardy Herbaceous and Alpine
Flowers, for General Garden Decoration. Containing Descriptions of upwards
of 1000 Species of Ornamental Hardy Perennial and Alpine Plants; along with
Concise and Plain Instructions for their Propagation and Culture. By WILLIAM
SUTHERLAND, Landscape Gardener; formerly Manager of the Herbaceous Depart-
ment at Kew. Crown 8vo, 7s. 6d.

TAYLOR. The Story of my Life. By the late Colonel
MEADOWS TAYLOR, Author of 'The Confessions of a Thug,' &c., &c. Edited by
his Daughter. New and Cheaper Edition, being the Fourth. Crown 8vo, 6s.

THOMSON.
The Diversions of a Prime Minister. By Basil Thomson. With a Map, numerous Illustrations by J. W. Cawston and others, and Reproductions of Rare Plates from Early Voyages of Sixteenth and Seventeenth Centuries. Small demy 8vo, 15s.

South Sea Yarns. With 10 Full-page Illustrations. Cheaper Edition. Crown 8vo, 3s. 6d.

THOMSON.
Handy Book of the Flower-Garden: Being Practical Directions for the Propagation, Culture, and Arrangement of Plants in Flower-Gardens all the year round. With Engraved Plans. By DAVID THOMSON, Gardener to his Grace the Duke of Buccleuch, K.T., at Drumlanrig. Fourth and Cheaper Edition. Crown 8vo, 5s.

The Handy Book of Fruit-Culture under Glass: Being a series of Elaborate Practical Treatises on the Cultivation and Forcing of Pines, Vines, Peaches, Figs, Melons, Strawberries, and Cucumbers. With Engravings of Hothouses, &c. Second Edition, Revised and Enlarged. Crown 8vo, 7s. 6d.

THOMSON. A Practical Treatise on the Cultivation of the Grape Vine. By WILLIAM THOMSON, Tweed Vineyards. Tenth Edition. 8vo, 5s.

THOMSON. Cookery for the Sick and Convalescent. With Directions for the Preparation of Poultices, Fomentations, &c. By BARBARA THOMSON. Fcap. 8vo, 1s. 6d.

THORBURN. Asiatic Neighbours. By S. S. THORBURN, Bengal Civil Service, Author of 'Bannú; or, Our Afghan Frontier,' 'David Leslie: A Story of the Afghan Frontier,' 'Musalmans and Money-Lenders in the Panjab.' With Two Maps. Demy 8vo, 10s. 6d. net.

THORNTON. Opposites. A Series of Essays on the Unpopular Sides of Popular Questions. By LEWIS THORNTON. 8vo, 12s. 6d.

TRANSACTIONS OF THE HIGHLAND AND AGRICULTURAL SOCIETY OF SCOTLAND. Published annually, price 5s.

TRAVERS.
Mona Maclean, Medical Student. A Novel. By GRAHAM TRAVERS. Eleventh Edition. Crown 8vo, 6s.

Fellow Travellers. Third Edition. Crown 8vo, 6s.

TRYON. Life of Admiral Sir George Tryon. By Rear-Admiral C. C. PENROSE FITZGERALD. With Portrait and numerous Illustrations. Demy 8vo, 18s.

TULLOCH.
Rational Theology and Christian Philosophy in England in the Seventeenth Century. By JOHN TULLOCH, D.D., Principal of St Mary's College in the University of St Andrews, and one of her Majesty's Chaplains in Ordinary in Scotland. Second Edition. 2 vols. 8vo, 16s.

Modern Theories in Philosophy and Religion. 8vo, 15s.

Luther, and other Leaders of the Reformation. Third Edition, Enlarged. Crown 8vo, 3s. 6d.

Memoir of Principal Tulloch, D.D., LL.D. By Mrs OLIPHANT, Author of 'Life of Edward Irving.' Third and Cheaper Edition. 8vo, with Portrait, 7s. 6d.

TWEEDIE. The Arabian Horse: His Country and People. By Major-General W. TWEEDIE, C.S.I., Bengal Staff Corps; for many years H.B.M.'s Consul-General, Baghdad, and Political Resident for the Government of India in Turkish Arabia. In one vol. royal 4to, with Seven Coloured Plates and other Illustrations, and a Map of the Country. Price £3, 3s. net.

TYLER. The Whence and the Whither of Man. A Brief History of his Origin and Development through Conformity to Environment. The Morse Lectures of 1895. By JOHN M. TYLER, Professor of Biology, Amherst College, U.S.A. Post 8vo, 6s. net.

VEITCH.
Memoir of John Veitch, LL.D., Professor of Logic and Rhetoric, University of Glasgow. By MARY R. L. BRYCE. With Portrait and 3 Photogravure Plates. Demy 8vo, 7s. 6d.
Border Essays. By JOHN VEITCH, LL.D., Professor of Logic and Rhetoric, University of Glasgow. Crown 8vo, 4s. 6d. net.
The History and Poetry of the Scottish Border : their Main Features and Relations. New and Enlarged Edition. 2 vols. demy 8vo, 16s.
Institutes of Logic. Post 8vo, 12s. 6d.
The Feeling for Nature in Scottish Poetry. From the Earliest Times to the Present Day. 2 vols. fcap. 8vo, in roxburghe binding, 15s.
Merlin and other Poems. Fcap. 8vo, 4s. 6d.
Knowing and Being. Essays in Philosophy. First Series. Crown 8vo, 5s.
Dualism and Monism ; and other Essays. Essays in Philosophy. Second Series. With an Introduction by R. M. Wenley. Crown 8vo, 4s. 6d. net.

VIRGIL. The Æneid of Virgil. Translated in English Blank Verse by G. K. RICKARDS, M.A., and Lord RAVENSWORTH. 2 vols. fcap. 8vo, 10s.

WACE. Christianity and Agnosticism. Reviews of some Recent Attacks on the Christian Faith. By HENRY WACE, D.D., Principal of King's College, London ; Preacher of Lincoln's Inn ; Chaplain to the Queen. Second Edition. Post 8vo, 10s. 6d. net.

WADDELL. An Old Kirk Chronicle : Being a History of Auldhame, Tyninghame, and Whitekirk, in East Lothian. From Session Records, 1615 to 1850. By Rev. P. HATELY WADDELL, B.D., Minister of the United Parish. Small Paper Edition, 200 Copies. Price £1. Large Paper Edition, 50 Copies. Price £1, 10s.

WALFORD. Four Biographies from 'Blackwood' : Jane Taylor, Hannah More, Elizabeth Fry, Mary Somerville. By L. B. WALFORD. Crown 8vo, 5s.

WARREN'S (SAMUEL) WORKS :—
Diary of a Late Physician. Cloth, 2s. 6d. ; boards, 2s.
Ten Thousand A-Year. Cloth, 3s. 6d. ; boards, 2s. 6d.
Now and Then. The Lily and the Bee. Intellectual and Moral Development of the Present Age. 4s. 6d.
Essays : Critical, Imaginative, and Juridical. 5s.

WENLEY.
Socrates and Christ : A Study in the Philosophy of Religion. By R. M. WENLEY, M.A., D.Sc., D.Phil., Professor of Philosophy in the University of Michigan, U.S.A. Crown 8vo, 6s.
Aspects of Pessimism. Crown 8vo, 6s.

WHITE.
The Eighteen Christian Centuries. By the Rev. JAMES WHITE. Seventh Edition. Post 8vo, with Index, 6s.
History of France, from the Earliest Times. Sixth Thousand. Post 8vo, with Index, 6s.

WHITE.
Archæological Sketches in Scotland—Kintyre and Knapdale.
By Colonel T. P. WHITE, R.E., of the Ordnance Survey. With numerous Illustrations. 2 vols. folio, £4, 4s. Vol. I., Kintyre, sold separately, £2, 2s.
The Ordnance Survey of the United Kingdom. A Popular
Account. Crown 8vo, 5s.

WILLIAMSON. The Horticultural Handbook and Exhibitor's
Guide. A Treatise on Cultivating, Exhibiting, and Judging Plants, Flowers,
Fruits, and Vegetables. By W. WILLIAMSON, Gardener. Revised by MALCOLM
DUNN, Gardener to his Grace the Duke of Buccleuch and Queensberry, Dalkeith
Park. New and Cheaper Edition, enlarged. Crown 8vo, paper cover, 2s.;
cloth, 2s. 6d.

WILLIAMSON. Poems of Nature and Life. By DAVID R.
WILLIAMSON, Minister of Kirkmaiden. Fcap. 8vo, 3s.

WILLS. Behind an Eastern Veil. A Plain Tale of Events
occurring in the Experience of a Lady who had a unique opportunity of observing the Inner Life of Ladies of the Upper Class in Persia. By C. J. WILLS,
Author of 'In the Land of the Lion and Sun,' 'Persia as it is,' &c., &c. Cheaper
Edition. Demy 8vo, 5s.

WILSON.
Works of Professor Wilson. Edited by his Son-in-Law,
Professor FERRIER. 12 vols. crown 8vo, £2, 8s.
Christopher in his Sporting-Jacket. 2 vols., 8s.
Isle of Palms, City of the Plague, and other Poems. 4s.
Lights and Shadows of Scottish Life, and other Tales. 4s.
Essays, Critical and Imaginative. 4 vols., 16s.
The Noctes Ambrosianæ. 4 vols., 16s.
Homer and his Translators, and the Greek Drama. Crown
8vo, 4s.

WORSLEY.
Poems and Translations. By PHILIP STANHOPE WORSLEY,
M.A. Edited by EDWARD WORSLEY. Second Edition, Enlarged. Fcap. 8vo, 6s.
Homer's Odyssey. Translated into English Verse in the
Spenserian Stanza. By P. S. Worsley. New and Cheaper Edition. Post 8vo,
7s. 6d. net.
Homer's Iliad. Translated by P. S. Worsley and Prof. Conington. 2 vols. crown 8vo, 21s.

YATE. England and Russia Face to Face in Asia. A Record of
Travel with the Afghan Boundary Commission. By Captain A. C. YATE, Bombay
Staff Corps. 8vo, with Maps and Illustrations, 21s.

YATE. Northern Afghanistan; or, Letters from the Afghan
Boundary Commission. By Major C. E. YATE, C.S.I., C.M.G., Bombay Staff
Corps, F.R.G.S. 8vo, with Maps, 18s.

YULE. Fortification: For the use of Officers in the Army, and
Readers of Military History. By Colonel YULE, Bengal Engineers. 8vo, with
Numerous Illustrations, 10s.

www.ingramcontent.com/pod-product-compliance
Lightning Source LLC
Chambersburg PA
CBHW020103030726
47498CB00006B/1920